Don't Smell _{The} Flowers! They Want _{To} Steal Your Bones!

A Cautionary Tale By
Duncan P. Bradshaw

EyeCue Productions 

ISBN – 978-1-999751265

Author Warning

Fig 1. The author and his attempt at 'research'.

This is Duncan P. Bradshaw. He is a silly man. Here he is taking a saw to a flower he was studying for the purposes of writing this book. It was brought to his attention that some people read his recent books and felt that they were far too ridiculous, and just wasn't what they expected.

To counter this, he has decided to place this warning at the front of this book, so you know exactly what you're getting into.

Look at his stupid face. If you think you can handle what that brain within his bulbous skull can throw at you, please continue. If not, you would be wise to bid adieu now.

This is your one and only warning. If you decide that you're up to be entertained by this moron, then that is on you.

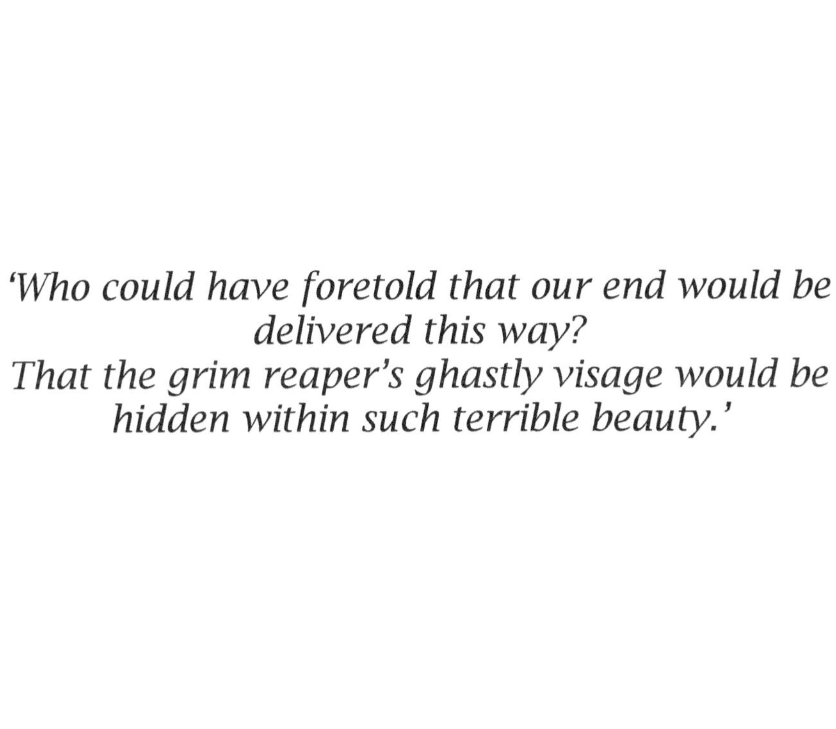

'Who could have foretold that our end would be delivered this way?
That the grim reaper's ghastly visage would be hidden within such terrible beauty.'

Chapter One

Eustoma grandiflorum

With a tissue wound around his finger, Chaz rubbed at the bird shit that had splattered down the front of his jacket. The scratching sounded like a cat's tongue rasping against dry skin, as he tried desperately to soak up the guano. "Don't lose your head over it. Remember, pebble in the stream…pebble in the stream." Overhead, a seagull cawed, surveying its handiwork, trying to muster another payload for a follow-up bombing run. Unable to contain it any longer, Chaz shouted at the bird. "Go on, get out of it, you little bleeder!" Realising it was going to be unable to repeat the feat down the other lapel, the bird screeched once more before banking sharply and heading out towards the town centre and the promise of ice cream cones and children with weak grasps.

Without thinking, Chaz licked his finger, eager to coat it in spit to try and help remove the troublesome stain. He grimaced as the taste of liquidised bird waste —comprising day-old chips and discarded salsa— left a nasty tang on his taste buds. As one of his eyes twitched, he tried once more to scritch and scratch the stubborn goo out of the weave.

Regarding his handiwork with a degree of resigned satisfaction, he smoothed down the lapel the best he could, before pulling up the handkerchief from the top pocket and draping it down like a depressed polka dot tongue to cover the stain. "First of the day," he pulled out a dog-eared notebook, jotting down: *Monday, #1 —bird poo. Again.*

Charlie 'Chaz' Thornton was known around the village as Lucky. A nickname in the same vein as those thieving wags in Robin Hood's band of merry men, deigning Little John so, because he was built like a brick shithouse. It wasn't done out of spite, but in the knowledge that no matter what Chaz did, despite the care he'd take, four acts of misfortune would befall him every day without fail.

In an attempt to try and get to the bottom of his predicament he had started to record his mishaps, inputting the accumulated data into a spreadsheet and using it to try and identify some hitherto undetermined pattern. So far, all he had concluded was that the local bird population seemed to have taken a shine to him. His current working theory was that perhaps his gait gave birds the impression he was a mobile latrine. He didn't know for sure, and why would he? Chaz was many things, but fluent in bird behaviour was not one of them. If he knew it was because the parting in his hair looked like a miniature albino snake, and the only way for a bird to scare such an animal off was to defecate on it, then he might have done something about it. Perhaps a change of haircut? A hat, maybe? Either way, even if he managed to stop the bird population crapping on him, you can bet your last extra strong mint that another denizen of the animal kingdom would step up to the challenge and endeavour to discharge their waste over the poor sod.

Scouting overhead, Chaz breathed a sigh of relief. The skies were clear. He checked the time again. Still a few minutes. He contemplated making a move now but considering the crowded bowels of the carrier bag between his feet, he decided he would wait a little longer, for his bad luck went beyond trivial acts such as resting against freshly painted bus stops or losing money down drains, and into his love life. His last girlfriend, Tina, had given him the elbow after Chaz accidentally set her ablaze on her birthday. In his defence, her chiffon dress was a known fire hazard, but most would think it impossible for birthday candle wax to cause an inferno. When he saw she was struggling to blow out her candles, he stepped up to the plate, closed his eyes, and doused the twenty-seven candles in a mix of fetid breath and saliva. In his gale force ten of keenness, he sprayed the errant wax over his beloved and she went up like an ant under a magnifying glass.

After that, he tried speed-dating, which ended abruptly after the first table when Emily pressed the poorly wired buzzer, sending the electrical charge directly into his right foot. He came to an hour later, face down in the alleyway out back with one numb leg and missing his shirt collar. The only thing in the plus column was that he still had both kidneys.

He fared little better with online dating, becoming the sole victim of a vicious hacking ring that changed his profile picture to that of a famous male model. "What's wrong with that?" you might ask. Nothing. Who wouldn't go for the owner of an animal sanctuary, with perfect teeth and rock-hard abs? Unfortunately, due to his new-found popularity, anyone swiping right was promptly delivered a not-so-flattering picture of Chaz's penis, procured via his webcam which had also been broken into by the fiends.

That had understandably dented his confidence, so it came as a complete surprise when the cashier down the Quantico-Mart had asked for his phone number. Chaz had already suffered his fill of bad luck for the day, so merrily skipped home, safe in the knowledge that the twisted deities of fate were done with fucking him over until midnight rolled around. He knew, though, that they would pay it back with interest, and ever since that day (three days earlier), Chaz had been paying particular attention to the hand dealt to him.

Eager to impress Natasha, he had gone a smidge overboard with gifts, all of which were currently testing the tensile strength of the plastic bag. The last thing he wanted was to put too much strain on it and spill the contents on the floor; something would undoubtedly trip one of them up and cause lasting injury —or even death. At best, untold psychological damage and trauma would befall one of them.

(It's possible. Trust me on that one —I speak from experience, when a Swiss roll fell out of my Bag for Life as I transported it back to my lair. No one died. It was just ruined. I'd been really looking forward to it and fell into a two-week funk.)

So Chaz was trying to time it to perfection, estimating that it would take him two minutes to traverse the distance from the bench he was currently perched on, past the crazy golf course and around the swings, before arriving in front of the window of the café. At best, he reckoned he could get three more minutes of pushing the plastic bag to its limits before the universe intervened and ballsed something up for him.

BONG!

The alarm he'd set failed in its usual fashion, trying to slip under his audio radar so he'd be late. The delay would make him flustered, careless, at the whim of the vagaries of fickle fortune. "Not today," Chaz said quietly, hoping to not piss off the balance of the world. Picking the bag up gingerly, he began to totter down the gravel path, stage one of his small trek underway.

Ahead and to the right, a couple were attempting hole eleven on the crazy golf course. It was a tricky one; of that there was no doubt. The shortcut —a difficult putt through a tramp's bowed legs, under a spinning blade and into a length of guttering which would catapult the ball at speed to the back half of the course— was made near impossible by the tramp convulsing after a bad wrap of cheap sherbet. Undeterred by the difficulty, there was the unmistakeable THWAP of metal against rubber as one of the contestants took their shot, followed by, "oh bollocking hell."

Evidently, the man taking the shot had failed to account for the effects of the whirling blade, and despite getting it through the tramp's legs, his gusto was for nought as the backdraft blew the ball all the way back to him, coming to a rest two feet behind where he'd taken the shot in the first place. "Oh dear, oh dear," His partner said, shaking her head, all the while trying to suppress a fit of the giggles.

"I knew I shouldn't have gone," the man whinged.

Chaz kept his head down, trying to not get pulled into a domestic which would undoubtedly spell doom for his bag of goodies. The woman chuckled as she plonked her ball down on the tee mark and did a little jiggle to set up, before hitting the ball perfectly. It whistled beneath the tramp's urine-stained crotch, rode the vortex of the blades, and broke the sound barrier as it flew through the tubing, before rattling in the hole at the end of the course.

The man squeezed the putter handle tighter, before his inner dam of resolve failed him spectacularly. "FUCKING BALLS TO YOU, MCCUNTY FUCKFACE," he shouted at the gaudily-painted windmill feature from hole ten.

The woman tucked her putter under her arm and marked her latest hole-in-one down on the scorecard. "Your turn, pumpkin. I'll let you take it again without marking down the shot, if you want?"

The man calmed a little, which was lucky for the fate of the poor orphan boy who had strayed onto the course, begging for scraps of Teflon so he could coat his rain mac for the coming autumnal months. "I fucking told you, I shouldn't have gone," the man complained once more.

"You really think it's to blame?"

Resting the ball on the mark, the man shimmied in the time-honoured way. "Of course I do. Look at the scores. Ever since I had that poo after the ninth hole, my game's gone to shit."

"Quite literally."

Still fuming, the man didn't even bother looking before taking a wild swing, the ball set on a collision course with Chaz. Fortunately, he'd been expecting it ever since he'd seen the couple start their round, and he turned towards the miniature cannon ball, taking it in the small of his back. Wincing, Chaz limped on, the man offering a weak but thoroughly genuine apology. All the while the woman laughed, relishing every minute of what had been quite a wonderful afternoon.

Setting down his burden, Chaz quickly scribbled in his journal. Two events in such quick succession was unusual, but not unheard of. Resuming his trek, he was resigned to the fact he'd be pissing blood for a week. The swings were next, both occupied with little children swinging happily away on them. They soared through the air like big-ass-motherfucking-swishy-blade-things; the kind you get in video games where you loot priceless heirlooms which had been left for millennia inside carefully constructed death-traps. He knew an impromptu shortcut was in order, so he'd picked out a spot ahead where he could skip the peril of taking a child's foot to the face and get to the café window unkicked.

All he had to do was cut through a row of tall, proud sunflowers.

What could possibly go wrong?

WELL?

Ah, right. Nothing. You're right. It's not as if the title of this book has anything to do with sunflowers, eh?

The stems were bunched together tightly, so Chaz had to lean into them and push his way through the dense foliage. Daring to look up to establish the position of the sun and make sure he was still on course, he saw the large flower heads loom over him like fiery eyes threatening to glare at him until the end of time itself. With every step through the floral domain, the flowers jiggled and shook; some started to bend over, their honeycomb faces coming close to rubbing themselves against him. There was a hissing sound as his polyester trousers rubbed against the dry stems.

Chaz was getting desperate. He felt like the flowers were closing in on him, hoping to disorientate him, spinning him round and round in their midst so he would lose all hope and succumb to apathy. Under their spell, he would fall to the soil and adopt the foetal position, allowing the flora to make short work of his organic matter, turning him to mulch so they could feed on his gooey insides.

As the first note of the panic symphony kicked in, Chaz felt fresh air against his cheek. Making himself look forward, he saw that he was free of the sunflower patch and was standing a few feet away from the café window —and from Natasha. Having escaped the clutches of the rustling flowers, Chaz dusted himself down, straightened the handkerchief over the shit stain, and walked the last few steps across to his date for the afternoon.

"Damn, she looks good." Only when Natasha blushed did he realise he had spoken out loud, and in a Northern accent, to boot. Embarrassed by both, he came to a halt. "I …erm …you know."

Natasha twirled on the spot, her fire-retardant dress —she had heard the stories and was taking no chances— brushing against her legs. "It's fine …thank you."

Lost in her words, Chaz stood rooted to the spot. Only the sound of stretching plastic brought him back to life. "Ah, hang on a minute. I have some things for you." He placed the bag on the ground.

"Some *things*? Plural?" Natasha asked, trying to sneak a peek.

"Oh, yes." Chaz rooted round the goodies to select his opening gambit, finally settling on the tried and trusted. "Here you go, hope you like them."

She took the box of chocolates and smiled, showing off her teeth. "I do. Thanks."

"I didn't know if you liked white chocolate, or milk chocolate, or dark chocolate."

"I like them all."

"Or truffles. Mint."

"Mmm, I love them all. Thanks."

"Toffee. Fudge. Popping candy."

Natasha pressed a finger against his lips. "I do, anything coated in chocolate is fine by me," She winked.

It was Chaz's turn to go red. With his brain having run out of possible chocolate combinations, he stood there like a powered down robot, before finally rebooting. "Anyway, that's not all."

"No?" There was a rustling, before Chaz stood up quickly; in his hand, a solitary orchid. "Wow, it's beautiful," Natasha murmured. She took the proffered flower gently, lest any pressure should destroy its beauty.

The stem itself was thick, like a jumbo drinking straw, and a large four-petal flower stood proudly on top of two green leaves, which acted like a split-skirt. The petals were arranged in a cross: three the same size and the top one double the size of its siblings. Each was a pale pink speckled with fine purple dots. So engrossed was she with the flower, that Natasha almost forgot about the chocolates.

Poking out of the middle of the flower were yellow stigmas, looking like a pair of jaundiced eyes on stalks. They twitched, as if trying to latch onto a radio signal and impart the latest traffic news. She could sense a gentle aroma from within the bulbous head, like freshly baked croissants resting on a plate by an open window. Just like mother used to make, so she could lure her errant daughter back inside after a long day of playing outside, liberating people of their gold doubloons.

Natasha locked her eyes on Chaz. "Thank you, it's so beautiful."

"Like you." Chaz's cheeks turned a deeper red as he reached into the bag once more. "Hang on, I've got some more stuff for you in here."

With eyes only for the orchid, Natasha pulled the flower in close so she could breathe in the scent of summers past. As soon as it encountered her nose, the stigmas retracted in what seemed like an insincere apology. The two balls inflated before exploding open, becoming a thrashing mess of tiny groping tentacles. They latched onto the sides of her nose, and try as she might, Natasha could not fight free of their hold.

Chaz's eyes were open wide; part-fear, part-wonder as the woman in front of him fought to keep the flower from engulfing her mouth and nose. Finally stirred into action, he dropped the next present —a framed picture of the Queen— and grabbed hold of her hands, trying to be chivalrous and save her from certain peril!

It was to no avail; the tendrils were too strong and would not be denied their prize.

Natasha felt the stem pulse through her fingers as the orchid upped its effort. Even with the assistance of Chaz, she could not stop the tentacles from pulling her nose into the flower head, each of the petals opening wide to accommodate the shape of her face, before closing and clinging to the contours of her skull. As it sealed up, there was an audible hiss and a cloud of orange particulate ejected from the miniscule gap by the bridge of Natasha's nose.

Chaz felt her fingers go limp before her entire body followed suit. He managed to catch her in his arms and laid her down gently.

By now, a small crowd had gathered around the unconscious woman. The crazy golfers considered administering an abrupt dose of vigilante justice but decided against it. Pulling out his notebook, Chaz wrote: *#3 — Date attacked and incapacitated by floral gift.*

Still shaking, he put the book and pen back in his pocket. *Least nothing worse can happen today.*

Just then, a pack of feral hedgehogs grabbed hold of his trouser legs and tugged, exposing to all and sundry that Chaz —in an attempt to minimise the effects of any and all potential trouser accidents— was wearing an adult nappy.

"Oh bugger," he managed, before collapsing to the ground, all four doses of bad luck having taken quite their toll.

Chapter
Two

Daucus carota

"If any of you pigs try to come in here, I'll slice your mate up into cubes of gammon." Pleased with managing to drop two references to swine and the police into one sentence, general ne'er do well and recent hostage taker, Ken Inglett kicked the door shut and retired back down the hallway, blade still pressed against PC Eric Rudgely's neck.

It was safe to say —and blindingly obvious— that Eric's first day on the job was not going terribly well. A simple check-up on Ken to ensure he had his 'Ne'er Do Well' license stamped and up-to-date, had led to him having a kitchen knife waved in his general direction. Fortunately, in the mayhem, he had at least managed to press his panic button, which was probably the only thing that had saved him from being discovered in a landfill site a few months down the line, his bloated body stuffed into an empty cornflakes box and riddled with beetles who just *loved* boring their way through dead human flesh.

Experienced negotiator and part-time wrist model Felicity Turnbull idly thumbed the button on the loudspeaker. She was eager to shout instructions to the cordon of police sharpshooters; specifically to PC Norman, who had just popped down the shops. When he'd asked, Felicity had said she didn't want anything, but now he'd had gone, she had developed a hankering for something sweet. She caved. "Oi, Norman, get us a Twix, will ya?" Her voice echoed down from the first-floor balcony. With a hand pushing against the newsagent's door, the constable shuddered from the noise, before turning around and offering a reluctant thumbs up.

"What are we going to do?" Felicity's voice boomed, as local wildlife turned and ran for their safe place, the woman's finger still holding down the loudspeaker trigger.

A little deafened, a generic cookie-cutter detective straight from the seventies pressed a hand on the megaphone, and the woman released her hold on the button. "The scrote is barricaded within a one-bed flat. Spotters out back report that he's closed all the curtains and pulled down his blackout blinds, so we can't see where he is. Thermal vision scopes are on the way, but they won't be here for a few hours yet. Before it went dark inside, our top looking-through-windows guy reported —"

Felicity gulped. "What? What did they report? Does he have an accomplice in there? Does he have access to public service radio to try and win the hearts and minds of the public?"

The detective twirled the end of his moustache and shook his head.

"Then what? What? TELL ME, DAMN YOUR EYES!" Even without the aid of amplification, people in the town of Andover, three miles away, were wondering what they should tell the demanding voice being carried aloft on the breeze.

"He's got gas tanks in there. Hundreds of 'em. If we try and take a shot, and miss —"

"My god —"

"Yeah, the whole block will go up. We'll be goners."

Felicity looked over the balcony towards the shop and the dillydallying PC Norman, desperate to get one of the chocolate-coated caramel fingers to calm her growing nerves. "Then what the hell can we do?"

"There's only one thing…or, should I say, one *person*, who can help us now."

"You don't mean? —"

The detective, because he was being written in a stereotypical and somewhat antiquated fashion, placed his thumbs behind his belt buckle and swayed on the spot. "Yep, Detective Harry Surge. He's the only one that can get young Rudgely out of there in one piece."

"But the man's a maniac, a loose cannon, a lone wolf, there's no way he'd help us out, not after —"

Sucking on a strawberry lollipop, the detective shirked Felicity's hand from his shoulder. "He can, and he will."

"But how do we even get hold of him? Isn't he serving another suspension?"

"Well…I know someone who knows someone, who petted this other bloke's dog, well, their owner? He went to school with Sandra, who got divorced from Mark. Anyway, he kept a matchbook from a plumbing job a few years back. In there? We found the first in a series of increasingly difficult riddles which took us on a path back in time to ancient Mesopotamia. Inside an underground fortress, guarded by the forces of eternal evil, we found Harry's pager number scrawled on the underside of a toilet plinth."

Felicity grabbed hold of the man's oversized collar, lifting him from the floor with ease. "You mean to tell me that the life of that young man, and potentially everyone on this estate, is resting on that pager number still being in use? IS THAT WHAT YOU'RE TELLING ME?"

You could cut the tension with a chubby finger —that's how thick it was; how laced with danger and trepidation. Squirming in the woman's powerful grasp, the detective nodded, the breath in his lungs insufficient to form words in his throat.

"Hey, if you two have finished dancing, would you mind stepping aside so some of us can do our goddamn jobs?" A deep voice boomed from the bottom of the walkway.

Turning as one, the pair looked at a man who looked like he had just got off a sunbed. Which wasn't a lie, as he actually had. The armed police who were guarding the stairwell trained their weapons on him before tutting and lowering them. Murmurs of, "fucking hell, it's *him*," formed into small cloud formations which would bring a brief downpour later on, between this chapter and the next.

"How did …" Felicity muttered.

A hand disappeared into the back of Tan-Man's Speedos, before rooting around for a good few seconds, every single one of them a year of awkwardness in real time. The closest firearm officer dared to look, before turning away and throwing up pink vomit over the balcony, covering his favourite trestle table below. Finally, Harry pulled his hand free. The abnormally brown hand —not all of which was as a result of the tanning session— held an old Motorola pager aloft, still vibrating the call for help in Morse code. "I got your message."

Tossing the buzzing device to another policeman, who juggled with it, desperate to not get any bum juice on his tactical gloves, Harry strode down the concrete walkway, dragging a covered trailer behind him. "You there, Big Jugs, give me a sitrep."

Felicity released the detective and looked around to see who the hell Harry was addressing before it dawned on her. "Do you mind? It's Detective Turnbull."

"I don't care if it's Queen Sweet Arse from the Planet Jiggly-Wiggly, tell me what we got. Time is a commodity we don't have, not when there are human lives on the line. They are human, aren't they? I'm not risking my neck for any more fucking cyborgs again. Not after last time."

"How dare you. I outrank you and this is my situation, so you will address me as—"

Harry held up a hand, coming to a stop a few feet in front of the negotiator, a whiffy tail of unpleasantness following in his wake. "You need me more than I need you. I was topping up the tan before getting a back, sack and crack sanding, so spare me the fake indignation —be a pro and tell me what we've got going down."

Felicity crossed her arms and pouted.

"Please." Harry added.

The pouting continued, now with additional toe tapping.

Harry held his hands together in mock prayer. "Fine, pretty fucking please with a jeroboam of Moet on top, can you tell me what's going on, or do I have to get the skinny from him?" He thumbed towards the detective, who was applying gel to his mullet.

Felicity sighed. "One hostage."

"One of ours?"

"Yep, standard license stamping, the target took exception to something."

"How many ways in or out?"

"One, not counting the windows, which the suspect has now covered."

"I heard on the blower that there are gas tanks in there. Hundreds of 'em."

"And they're everywhere. Look, we have equipment coming in, but it won't be here for a while. I've got a bad feeling about this. We need to get PC Rudgely out of there. Fast. Will you help?"

Harry peeled off his sunglasses, leaned backwards and sucked in as much air as he could store. At capacity, he allowed himself to deflate slowly, before slinging his shades back on and activating his favourite nonchalant shrug. "But of course. Though there is one thing I'll be needing."

"What?"

He sidled up to the woman and ran a drying, shitty finger down her cheek. "When this is all over, me and you go to the new Italian downtown, *Molto Benny*. Garlic bread, antipasti, pizza, maybe later you get your teeth into the meatballs?" He pulled out two strips of paper from his vacuous sphincter. "I have vouchers."

Felicity slapped him hard across the cheek, the sound like a starter's pistol which made the array of heavily armed police officers twitchy. To his credit, Harry managed to keep his sunglasses on and the vouchers held aloft. He shrugged. "I'll take that as a maybe. I dig. You want to see what I've got first, that's only fair. You there, do you have the perp's file?"

After straightening his kipper tie, the detective passed across a manila folder. Harry flipped it open and leafed through each and every morsel of information contained within. PIN numbers, acquaintances, the number of times Ken had partaken in hot tub sessions in the last nine months, what type of horse he'd be, and his bedtime habits. Harry closed the file and handed it back. Adjusting his crotch, he gave Felicity a mock salute with his penis. "Best stand back now, Missy, it's time to get the magic started."

Ken loomed over PC Rudgely. The scar that ran from forehead to groin puckered as the man scowled. "Do what I bloody well tell you to, boy."

"Please, no. I can't."

Turning the blade this way and that to catch the candlelight dramatically, Ken chuckled. "Oh, dearie dearie me, what did they teach you in pig academy?"

"Huh?"

"If you get taken hostage, don't you have to obey the demands put upon you?"

Eric was shaking vigorously, beads of sweat spraying over the flocked carpet. "They did…but this…I just can't. Please don't make me."

Ken turned and hurled the knife at a conveniently-placed dartboard on the far wall. With a THUNK, it landed right in the bullseye, a feat both men acknowledged with a smile. "Don't make me hurt you, *boy*."

"I'm not saying it to displease you, it's just a physical impossibility."

Squeezing his shaved head with one hand, Ken waved the piece of square cardboard at the policeman who was on all fours in a reverse plank position. "Left hand, green."

Casting a glance at the Twister mat beneath him, Eric shuddered. "It's all the way over there. I can't reach, I'll never make it."

Ken crouched down, his face inches from Eric's. "How do you know unless you try, Eh?"

"I just know. Please, I don't want to pull a muscle. I've got a half-marathon next week."

The hostage taker loped across to the dartboard and yanked the knife free. "If you don't, I'm going to cut off your left hand and PUT IT ON GREEN."

"Okay, okay. I'll give it a go." Eric panted, trying to centre himself. With enough courage built up (finally), he flung out his left hand and slapped it on the green circle. After a hairy moment when he almost slipped onto his backside, he pushed himself up. "I did it, I bloody did it."

Ken clapped, forgetting he was still holding the knife, and lopped off the tip of a middle finger. "I told you, didn't I? Now, let's see what's next." Using the tip of the bloodied blade, he spun the plastic pointer. As it came to a stop, he smiled and looked up. "Right hand, green."

"You have got to be kidding—" The front window rattling in its frame cut the copper off. Ken raised a hand for silence, which was a bit unnecessary as an unusual noise such as this will shut most people up on its own.

"Shh," Ken added, equally unnecessarily.

Straining towards the window, which was covered by a thick curtain, Eric's mouth fell open. "Did you hear that? It sounded like a child's voice."

"Impossible. The filth would've cleared everyone out of the block by now."

"Listen. Shh." PC Rudgely added, keen to join in the telling-people-to-be-quiet game.

Ken tiptoed towards the large window, which would've looked out onto the walkway if only it wasn't shut off from the world by the hastily-arranged bedsheet barricade. As he got closer, he heard it again.

"Are you in there, Kenny?" A shrill young voice called out.

"No way." Ken marched to the window and crouched beneath it. "Is it really you?"

There was a hushed exchange outside before the child's voice replied, "It is me. Ratko, the poor orphan boy you rescued from the ice cream man's van in Skopje last year."

Ken sunk to the floor, legs splayed out as if he were about to give birth. "Impossible…"

"After you saved me, the authorities took me in. Knowing that my parents were killed by the same madman that imprisoned me in that chest freezer, they sent me here to recover from the terrible things forced upon me."

His head slumped forward, narrowly missing the tip of the knife, which would've ended the hostage situation prematurely. "But how…how did you find me?"

"I didn't. The nice policeman out here found me. He went through your file, found the newspaper cuttings, made a few calls —and by chance, I was begging for change under Second-Chance Bridge."

"You mean? …"

"Yes. After all this time, we were separated by mere miles, maybe even metres. Or feet, depending on your preference for metric or imperial measurement." There was a slap of hand against skin, followed by a terse whispered exchange. A nervous cough shook the windowpane once more. "I mean…capricious fate has drawn us —"

Another solid slap ended the sentence. Ken squeezed the knife hilt. "You better not be hurting him out there, or so help me …"

Turned up to full volume, Harry's amplified voice boomed through the wall, almost making Ken soil himself. "Come on, we can work this out. All you have to do is release PC Rudgely, then I can make all of this go away."

Ken looked across at his hostage, who was doing his best to keep rooted to the coloured spots on the PVC mat. "Fine. But before I agree to anything, I wanna see him. I wanna see little Ratty."

"Fine. Just open the curtain, Ken. Open it up, he's right outside."

"You better not be messing with me. Remember, I've got all these lovely gas cannisters in here, one of your pig shooters tries ventilating my brain, we all go BOOM-BIDDY-BYE-BYE."

"We know. Please, Ken. Let's work this out. Open the curtains. Look upon little Ratko, see how much he's grown. The rickets have all but subsided, he can stand up straight now. The ice cream headaches have stopped. He's a medical marvel, all thanks to your bravery and foresight."

Grabbing hold of the nearest gas tank, Ken shoved the knife in the back of his belt, held the tank to his chest and stood up. "Fine, I'm going to open the curtain now."

"Just wait till you see him, you can actually see his face now. All the soot has been cleaned off, and he only has one large pustule left. Though that might just be his nose. It's pretty huge."

Clutching the weighty tank to his chest, Ken fumbled to yank the curtain open with his free hand. With his fingers curled round the hem, he did so in one fluid motion. "Huh? Where's little Ratty?"

Standing the other side of the single pane window was not a rejuvenated Balkan orphan boy. Not even close. Instead there was a patchily tanned man in a ridiculously tight pair of speedos, with only a wristwatch and a pair of sunglasses offering anything in the way of clothing. He uttered four words. "Hey, fuckhead. Heads-up." Ken looked in disbelief as the man tossed a megaphone to a colleague and stood to one side, revealing a one-third scale trebuchet, primed, loaded and ready to fire.

"Bugger," Was all Ken could muster before Harry pulled the release and a chunk of breeze block was launched through the window, catching the perp square in the upper chest. The force sent him sprawling backwards as the gas tank - unbreached but for a large dent - rolled to one side.

Lying on his back, Ken could feel a beautiful lightness in his chest. The lower half of his body felt warm and wet. He dabbed at his belly button, prodding at what he thought could only be a crystalline lake, and held his fingers in front of his face. Instead of cool aqua, his fingers were stained red.

"Fucking hell, that's some bad luck right there." Harry leaned over, removing his sunglasses to look down better at the stricken man.

"Are you…are you Jesus?" Ken asked.

Harry crouched down and patted the man on the cheek with his poo-covered mitt. "Afraid not, my Pedigree Chum. I'm the man they call to get shit done, and you my fucked-up friend, are the shit. That I've just done."

Ken chuckled and showed Harry his dripping fingers. "You turned water into wine!"

Knocking the hand to one side, Harry lifted Ken's head. "You dozy sod, that's not wine, it's blood. *Your* blood. Look." While still gripping Ken's hair like a bowling ball, he pointed a spare finger at the hostage taker's groin. A single metal mountain rose from the place his bladder was. "Looks like you took a tumble onto your blade. What fucking numbskull puts a knife in their belt?"

Ken tapped his chest. "Me?"

"It would appear so. You really are a dumb fuck."

Hoiking up a chewy clump of blood, Ken beckoned Harry closer. "Please…where's Ratty? Let me see him…before I go."

"Of course. Hang on a minute."

The near-naked detective turned to leave, before spinning back round. Adopting the disembodied child's voice, he squeaked, "You really are a fucking idiot. What kind of complete and total buttock-wearing arsehole would genuinely think that the kid they saved from some backwater shithole a year ago would appear here out of the blue?"

"Me?"

"That's right. Look, I'm bored of this now. If you're lucky, the paramedics will save you. If not, you're going to bleed out on this excuse for a carpet. Either way, I am outta here, loser." Harry let go of Ken's head —which smacked against the floor with exactly the kind of splat you're imagining right now. He strode to the doorway, where Felicity was blocking the way. "There you go, Bambino. One dipshit, bagged and tagged. Now how about some crudités?"

Felicity held out a detective badge, which swung from a navy-blue lanyard. "I've got something else for you. If you're interested?

Harry danced from foot-to-foot, scratching his head like a monkey. "Lookie here, Pa. The lady from the big building has got a job for me, YEE-HAW. Give me a goddamn reason why I should help you out, princess?"

"This new situation is a strange one—last time I checked you were all about the weird stuff. Didn't you break up that cabal of international apostrophe smugglers?"

Harry quit his tomfoolery, made the trebuchet safe, and pulled a burlap sheet over the siege weapon. "It would have to be grade-A category weird shit to get me to stick around here. I've got some intense manscaping waiting for me back at the Spa. You know, the one I'm moonlighting at until this latest complaint is swept under the carpet? Until you crapped your apple-catchers, that is, and I came-a-running to bail you out."

The woman waved the badge in front of him. "Trust me, you've never seen anything like this. No-one has."

"I'll be the judge of that," Harry sighed, picking up the rope which led to the trebuchet trailer. "What is it?"

Letting Harry snatch the detective badge from her, Felicity pushed past him into the flat. "Get down to the hospital, you'll see."

Chapter
Three

Limonium platyphyllum

"A flower?" Harry asked, pulling his sunglasses off and tucking them into the front of his groin-hugging swimming pants.

Dr. Singh was scribbling down notes. "To all intents and purposes, that's what it looks like, but I've never seen anything like it." He flipped through the pages on his clipboard, every single word and sentence he forced himself to look at was nonsensical, until he realised that someone had swapped the patient information with an Australian takeaway menu. "Ah, no wonder the words are all upside down."

"I get it, this is some kind of practical joke, isn't it? Ha ha, big laugh at the hotshot detective, let's send him down the hospital as someone has hay fever."

"It's not hay fever, it's some kind of…thing."

"*Thing?*"

"That's correct."

"Come on, Doc, throw me a fucking bone here, will ya? It may look like I'm on a jolly, but I really do have better things I could be doing. Police things, you know? Failing that, Beryl offered me some liposuction earlier, said it might help to drain my massive fucking bollocks. A danger to humanity, she called them."

Singh gestured towards a sealed door. "It'll be easier if you see for yourself."

"Before we do, where's the suspect? I heard they brought him in here. Is he handcuffed to a radiator or something? Can I kick the shit out of him?”

“I don't think he'll be any use to you, not in the state they found him in. Anyway, he's in surgery.”

“What for?”

The doctor checked a large whiteboard. “Penis enlargement, by the looks of it. Ah, this must be the kid they found with a swarm of hedgehogs keeping his trousers down.”

Harry sniggered. “Knob-extension? Ha! Mind you, I get enough of the emails for some reason. Tell me, what does the procedure entail?”

On the back of a piece of important documentation relating to Cynthia Bottomley's ovaries —the patient in cubicle eight if you're interested, though she doesn't appear again in this book— Singh drew an outline of the human form. “It's a simple skin graft. We'll use this,” He said, circling the right leg.

“You'll shave some of the skin off and use it to pack the old chap up, transforming into an even bigger danger to underpants elastic?”

Singh laughed. “Not at all, how primitive. No, we'll remove the leg and transplant it onto his penis.”

“And what will you do with the leg you've just hacked off?”

“We replace it with the penis, give it a bit of a stretch, then pack it out with some duck feathers and polystyrene balls. Very tastefully done,” Dr. Singh sang, finishing off his borderline pornographic picture with a flourish. Signing it in the corner, he handed it to Harry, completely bypassing the stringent rules on patient confidentiality.

“Okay, I wish I never asked, let's go see the girl.”

After swiping a key card through an electronic reader, which resulted in a green light and a satisfying BING, the Doctor led Harry into the room. No sooner had the detective pulled his trebuchet through the doors than they lazily closed behind him. The room was set up for two beds, only one of which was occupied. A thick opaque plastic sheet was pulled round it, stealing the view of the bed's occupant from the pair.

Harry frowned. “This seems a bit overkill for someone who's got a thorn stuck in a thumb or something, good to see my hard-earned tax wonga being chucked away in epic style.”

Singh pulled open the corner of the sheet a touch. “Please, go in.”

Leaving his trebuchet outside, a scowling Harry brushed past the man. One thing he hated more than anything —even more than pedestrians not using their indicators whilst turning into the newsagents— was having his time wasted. Feeling the bed sheet against his leg, Harry turned slowly before he uttered, “Fucking. Hell.”

Natasha was laid out in bed. Her arms were by her side, uncovered, and wires and monitors were slapped on any piece of exposed skin the nurse could find. That was pretty standard hospital fare; Harry had seen it before and he'd undoubtedly see it again, especially in his line of work. It was the woman's face that caused him to drop another F-bomb. Her eyes were closed gently, as if sleeping; if it wasn't for the flower stuck to the lower half of her face, you'd wonder what the hell she was doing in hospital. "Is that thing real?" Harry asked, his legs barely letting him stumble to the head of the bed.

"It is indeed." Dr. Singh was on the other side of the patient, stethoscope breathed on and primed, he killed some time by checking for a pulse.

Harry bent over the woman, his nose twitching. "What is that smell? It's like…"

"Freshly procured dog lactations swirling gently in a metal bowl." Singh replied, without looking up.

"No, that's just weird. It's more like gently heated Madagascan Vanilla custard. Bubbling away on the stove."

A creepy voice from the doorway made both men jump. "How about you're both right, but also both wrong?"

With balled-up fists, Harry pushed his way past the plastic sheet and into the room. Greeting him there was a plump man in a Tuxedo and morning jacket, complete with top hat and cane. He twiddled the end of an immaculate, pencil-thin moustache, his monocle gleaming from the overhead lights. Touching the brim of his hat, the man pushed his weight off the cane —which was dug into the floor— and walked forward. "Good afternoon, gentlemen, what a fine day it is indeed. Pray tell, what do you make of the afflicted young lady over yonder?"

Dr. Singh switched into diagnosis mode. "The patient is non-responsive to external stimuli; nothing, not even the strongest of slaps has been able to stir her from her catatonic state."

"And what do you make of her new appendage?" The gentleman enquired.

Singh prodded it with the end of his biro. "It has covered the entirety of her breathing apparatus. I'd speculate that the aim of the flower is not to kill, but to incapacitate, as it appears to be allowing her to breathe, either through it, or through some kind of membrane we have yet to name."

Flipping back to Natasha, Harry grabbed hold of the stem, which was warm to the touch. Holding it, he could feel it pulse —as if it were swallowing. Gently at first, he began to tug on it. The hold on the woman's face was total. Despite applying more pressure, the petals clung to the side of the face with ease. As tiny gaps appeared at the joining of the petals, the smell of custard grew stronger. "Perhaps I could give it a quick blast with the trebuchet? I'm sure it wouldn't be so keen on sticking to her face then." Harry went to pull the sheet free of the weapon, when Monopoly man placed a hand on the detective's.

"I think not. Even if your aim were true, it would not remove it from the fair maiden. You would be more likely to cave in her skull than free her of her predicament."

Harry shirked the man's hand off and pushed him backwards. Edging closer to the stranger, he noticed that the skin on the man's face appeared to ripple. Thinking it a mere trick of the light, Harry shook his head. "Who the fuck are you?" He glanced over at the door which was firmly closed. "And how did you get in here?"

Removing his top hat, exposing slicked-down hair which looked drawn-on, the man bowed shallowly. "I, good Sirs, am Barnaby. I am intimately familiar with the genus of that particular flora. When I heard that it had afflicted a lady, I made my way here post-haste."

Harry pressed a finger into the man's ribcage, which bulged inwards as he dug the digit farther in. "And the door?"

"It was open. Or at least it was when I stood in front of it." Barnaby fluttered his eyelashes. Harry looked into the man's eyes. The white bits were *really* white, as if they'd been bleached; the iris looked drawn-on with layers of felt-tip pen. And he could detect a slight whiff of vinegar.

"A likely story. I think you'd better do one before I arrest you for all the unsolved cases back at the station."

Barnaby stepped forward, the detective's finger disappearing deeper into the man's bulbous chest. "I will retire, for now. But mark my words, you will require my assistance before this day is through. This village, and maybe the entire *county* is in grave peril."

"Yeah, I bet, from you and your child-catcher net, probably."

Grinning, Barnaby extricated the detective's hand from his upper torso, which slowly reinflated to its usual shape. With one hand clutching Harry's, he slid his free hand into an inside pocket and retrieved two items, which he pressed into Harry's palm. "There isn't much time, I'm afraid. Here is a little something to assure you of my sincerity." Plonking his top hat back on his head, he struck the top with his cane, before rapping it twice on the floor. "Good day, Detective Surge. I'll be seeing you presently." With that, Barnaby tottered back to the door, which opened as he approached.

"What a strange man," Dr. Singh remarked, walking back to the patient.

Harry opened his hand. In his palm were a creased business card and an abnormally large bourbon cream biscuit, individually wrapped. The card merely confirmed the man's identity, seemingly in the Madonna mould; aside from a local telephone number, the card only bore his first name, Barnaby. The card itself smelt of formaldehyde, with a faintly-etched coffin as a background. Shoving it in his inside pocket —you know, his bum— Harry ripped open the biscuit wrapping. Ordinarily, he would devour said baked good whole, but given its size, he snapped it in two. Both halves sagged but did not part. Annoyed that the free biscuit was giving him shit, he pulled it apart. As he did, he found a folded piece of paper sticking out of the chocolate cream centre.

Shoving one half of the bourbon in his mouth, he pulled the paper from the cream and smoothed it out. "What the hell is this?"

"Looks like some kind of alternative fortune cookie?"

"Maybe, but this is no fortune."

Dr. Singh peered over the detective's shoulder. "Looks like a page from someone's diary."

"But whose?"

14 August 1682

It has been a day of much strangeness. The aubergines in the lower allotment pulled themselves out of their dirt moorings with ease, and if it were not for Damian, my formidable black cat, then I fear they would have made it all the way to the Wiltshire border.

Then, after looping vegetable anchors around the wayward plants and securing them back in the ground, a terrible roar from the depths of the forest caused all six of my hens to call out seventeen times before they all succumbed to a peculiar sickness. The most devilish symptoms were when their legs fell off and both halves of each beak melted into one long singular beak. Although they were useful for breaking open small rocks to obtain the bounty within, they were unable to feed and died shortly before nightfall.

Alas, with the losses of the day, I must forage for suitable provisions in the early hours of the morrow. Fresh mandrake root, chubby red mushrooms, chinchilla claws and a decent cumulative length of nubile five-legged stench grub will be needed. And quickly, lest the spirits of this haunted dale be fully awoken. Who knows what ills would befall this place —my home, if their mischievous whims are not catered to?

I know this for certain. The local villagers would once more cast their aspersions on me. I was —narrowly— able to avoid their accusations last time, yet more of their slander and fearmongering may expend what little remaining fortune I have, and I will be forced to submit to their trials.

Then it would be a matter of having to decide upon which fate I should embrace. Perhaps I should look to discover their true intentions?

Harry turned the paper over. He could feel warm breath against his neck and elbowed Dr. Singh, who was camped in his personal space. "This is police business, keep your nose out of it."

"What do you think was going on?"

"Who knows? And right now, I couldn't give a low-flying fuck. I'm gonna head home, change into some proper clothes, and give the trebuchet a buff-up. Let me know if you have any information on Triffid-face, okay?"

The doctor let the detective out through the doors —which patently refused to open without the required key card— before returning to his favourite pastime of staring vacantly at patients and wondering if he possessed any dormant psychic skills which could be used to heal.

Or KILL!

He'd work out if he'd use his power for good or evil on a case-by-case basis. "Always good to keep your options open," He told the comatose woman. That was his second favourite pastime. Talking to people who didn't answer back or judge him for his potentially psychotic views.

Chapter
Four

Matthiola incana

Twirling the spoon clockwise seventeen times before slowing to a crawl and resuming the stirring anti-clockwise, Wonky Tab finally ceased, content that the sugar had fully dissolved. Making tea is an exact science; mark my words, if you don't believe me, try drinking one with sugar which hasn't been stirred properly. First off, you'll wonder if you'd forgotten to put any in at all, until you get to the bottom half-inch and develop type two diabetes.

Sat on a park bench dedicated to the street urchins who had given their lives in the Battle of Foxcote Hill the previous year, Wonky wiped a tear from his eye, careful to not disturb his meticulously applied face paint. "This is for you, bruv. Taken too soon, innit." Wonky had been friends with the late Booyah Bojangles —real name Ben Miles— since they were knee-high to a grasshopper. Which is a stupid saying. Let's just say that they were both little people, around five years old in human years, when one gave the other head lice. I don't know which one was the carrier, but it wiped out most of the class.

Booyah wasn't the first nickname he had been blessed with. Like most boys, he had a long and illustrious history of monikers. The first one that stuck, and which took the most time to grow out of, was Beh Milse. Subtle perhaps, but it was the one that hurt the most. He had misspelt his name once on the back of a picture at school and the kids had taken every opportunity to remind him. They were eight years old! Did you know what dyslexia meant when you were eight? Fuck, I was writing letters to my teacher in orange felt tip pen, trying to swing my way out of swimming as I feared I'd die in the chlorinated water, signing off with 'Love Mummy', and wondering why Mrs Smith laughed and told me I was going to have double swimming for the sheer temerity to try and get out of it.

Anyway, Beh Milse loved nothing more than painting, not stuff you'd consider works of art —don't forget, he was only a kid— but he was meticulous in every detail but one. First, he would sketch the subject in pencil, before outlining it in thick black marker. Then, with all his favourite paints lined up, he'd go all over the lines he'd painstakingly made. He loved it. Wonky Tab did not. It drove him loopy. So now, twenty years later, as he stood over the chalk outline of his friend, with Booyah's now-dried blood having refused to stay within the neat white lines, Wonky's brain replayed images of his chum slapping oodles of paint on the page as if he was suffering from hand tremors. He was an annoying little shit, even in death.

Still, he wasn't here to let that get to him, not too much, anyway. This moment was all about paying respect to his fallen brother-in-arms. They'd grown up in the hood; and by hood, I mean a council estate just down the road from Charlton village, those hazy summer days daring to venture into their rival gang's turf on their bikes, turning tail when confronted by other oiks and lobbing water balloons behind them as they fled back to their home ground.

But that was then, and this is now. Those trivial times gave way to more serious showdowns. They thought that by moving to the village they would be free, but once you're in, you can't get out of the life —it'll always find you. In this case, it found Booyah as he was drinking a cuppa on his favourite bench, a slice of Bakewell tart resting on a plate next to him. Wonky knew who had taken his friend out, the rival Skinny Latte gang, hopped up on cream and caffeine. Being part of the Tea Boys, Wonky and Booyah would often partake in drive-bys at the local coffee shops, flinging tea bags at the windows, smearing tea leaves on the top of door handles, the usual hijinks. Retribution usually followed: frothy milk left on doorsteps in the heat, causing an awful pong, coffee essence being injected into ice lollies, but nothing on this scale. No-one had ever been killed over their choice of hot beverage. Mutilated for life, maybe, but until now, all had been fair in life, brewing and percolation.

Wonky heard how the Skinny Lattes had encircled Bojangles, castigating him for his choice of drink and mugging him right off over his selection of cake. He could almost hear his friend's fateful last words hanging in the air. "I bet you prefer granules over actual beans, you fake ass coffee dickheads." An eyewitness told the cops that the Skinny Lattes had become enraged shortly after Bojangles was seen making a T with his hands, the gang sign that sealed his fate. They took out their cafetière plungers, and before common sense could rein them in, they went for Booyah, plunging him over and over again. His body was perforated with over eighteen puncture wounds, and hundreds of scratches. The Latte's hybrid blend of dark and medium roast beans still laced their implements.

They weren't to know about Booyah's coffee intolerance, or that his way of life wasn't down to snobbery, but necessity. It wasn't the negligible wounds that had killed him, but the traces of Columbian coffee that ran through his bloodstream like a streaker at a cricket match.

It had thinned his blood, which in turn slopped out of the puncture wounds like skimmed milk, refusing to dry quickly and ruining the later attempt at drawing an exact marker around the corpse when the cops turned up.

Oh, and making Booyah bleed to death in a little under nine minutes, of course.

(Must remember which is the more pertinent of those two points when recounting this tale.)

Wonky held the cup of tea up high and closed his eyes. "Booyah. We brewed together, we strained together. Brew well, dawg. Brew well." With that, he poured the tea onto the ground, the tannin mixing with the blood, the concoction running down into the cracks of the pavement, destroying crucial forensic evidence.

What a knobhead.

Allowing himself a moment of introspection, Wonky tapped the bottom of the cup to empty every last drop out, before putting it into his man bag. Zipping it shut, he was all set to turn homewards, get the kettle on and get himself a nice cup of Indonesian Fhu-Ka tea on the go, when he caught a whiff of something.

It was bergamot. It was tree bark. It was hibiscus and anise.

It was heaven.

But where was it?

Eyeing up the ground, Wonky knelt and took a sniff of the tea-and-blood mix before recoiling, glad it was not the source. He wanted it — whatever it was— inside him. Flowing down his throat into his gullet, where it would be digested over a hundred years. Well, around ten or twenty minutes —it's tea, for heaven's sake, not a sarlacc living inside the Great Pit of Carkoon.

If it wasn't coming from there, where *was* it coming from? Forgoing social convention, Wonky stomped around the bench, sniffing deeply, in danger of blacking out through said peculiar breathing method which was starving his stupid brain of oxygen. As the world began to go inverted, turning black to white and vice versa, his head brushed past the floral tribute that had been left for Bojangles.

It was there. He knew it. Somewhere amongst the array of flowers was the prize —and, by Jove, he would claim it as his own. Incurring the wrath of the family of the recently deceased and others who had spent their hard-earned cash on the dead flower offerings, Wonky began to work through them one by one. He'd grab them within his tight fists, take a whiff, swear, then discard the flower to one side. Until, that was, he pulled one large-headed flower to his face.

By that point, he was wondering if he'd hallucinated the smell. As a teenager he'd believed he could smell fish living in the cavity walls, going so far as to smash through the plaster, trying to save the captive piscine. Alas, all he got for his troubles was a clip round the ear from his father, lessons in how to repair damage to plasterboard, and a doctor's appointment which uncovered the root of the malaise —an infected testicle. One bollock less, the stench of trapped fish had gone, and he had more room in his underpants, which he utilised in later life to store emergency tea bags —and his favourite sterling silver spoon.

Wonky collapsed back onto the bench and regarded the flower. It was an odd one; the stem was thick and chunky like a stick of seaside rock. He held it upside down and could see that it was hollow, but despite squeezing hard, it didn't surrender to the pressure. The petals fluttered, as if caught on a breeze. For a moment, it looked like they were reaching for him. "Madness," he said. The stigmas writhed, tempting him forward as if they were a potential suitor, hoping for some smooth docking action.

The movement was odd —creepy, almost, and if it wasn't for that alluring scent, he would've thrown it away, stamped on it probably, made his way home and forgotten all about it. But that would make this part of the story pointless and unnecessary; you wouldn't be best pleased if that happened —and I can't say I'd blame you.

As the tendrils waved the aroma towards the man, he gave in. Closing his eyes, he pulled the flower close and took a deep sniff. No sooner had his nose invaded the petal sanctum than they closed around his mouth and nose, seeking to cover the breathing holes. The tentacle-like stigmas wormed up into the nostrils, their tiny barbs holding onto the moist warmth within and pumping their neurotoxins into the bloodstream.

Wonky barely even knew what had happened; he had already slumped backwards, unconscious, the flower jutting from his face like an upside-down snorkel.

Taking a shortcut back home, Harry walked up Foxcote Hill. Cutting down the path at the back of Dacre Close would mean he could shave two, maybe three seconds off his journey time. As he neared the crest of the hill, he saw the bench that served as the marker of boundaries between the hipster beverage gangs.

This summer had been one of the most brutal on record; nineteen were hospitalised with a variety of injuries ranging from teabagging to scalds and burns. There had even been one fatality, whose aftermath Harry had witnessed, stepping barefoot through the puddles of blood and ruining the neat lines of white and crimson.

His heart skipped a beat as he saw a figure collapsed on the bench, head towards the cloudless sky, a green rod protruding from the nose. "Oh god, no. NO!" Harry ran over and felt for a pulse, and fist-pumped when he found it was strong. With no Doctor around to ask questions, and the CCTV cameras disabled, Harry rooted around in the man's pockets. It was rent day tomorrow, and he was still short of the required amount that Skullcrusher Sandra demanded, plus a vig by way of compensation.

"How wonderful to see you here, detective."

Harry screamed as the words were near whispered into his ear. He leapt backwards before jumping up in a Kung Fu stance. Stood in front of him was Barnaby, still as formally dressed as before, and still as fucking weird. "What are you doing here?"

Barnaby tittered into his gloved hands, hiding the lower part of his face. Just before it got too annoying, he stopped. "Where else would I be, detective?"

"I dunno. Back in the asylum for mentally deranged nutjobs?"

With an unorthodox sliding motion, Barnaby lurched towards Harry, coming to rest toe-to-toe with the man. "Oh, that's good. I suppose my appearance is the reason for this verbal insult?"

"Well yeah. Look at ya, you look like a really obvious bad guy who's been rejected for being too stereotypical."

Removing his hat, Barnaby bowed deeply, maintaining eye contact as he did so; there was a cracking and crunching as his head defied logic. Standing swiftly upright, Barnaby plunged his hand inside his jacket. "You know what I'm doing here, detective. I'm here to help. Here." The plastic-wrapped Rich Tea biscuit was out of the jacket interior and into Harry's hand before he even had a chance to acknowledge the movement. The man gently closed Harry's fingers around it, placing a digit on the detective's lips. "Shh."

"Thanks?"

"You're welcome." Barnaby relinquished his grip and went to walk down the hill.

"Hang on, is this another diary biscuit?"

"One side of a coin would say that it is, whilst the other would swear blind that it's not."

"It is, though, isn't it?"

Barnaby came to a stop, the sole of his shoes squeaking loudly against the ground. "Yes."

"What's it all about?"

"Why don't you open it up and see?"

Harry pointed the biscuit at the man, his free hand groping behind him for the sheet covering the trebuchet. "How about you just fucking tell me? Eh? Save us all a load of time and effort, and just say?"

"What would be the point in that? The chase would not be as enjoyable if the prey was pounced upon at the beginning. The cheese would not be so, if you tired of waiting and simply drank the milk. The—"

Harry held a hand up. "Alright, calm down, Riddler. Fucking hell. Seriously, what am I supposed to do with this?" He waved the biscuit at Barnaby —who shrugged.

"You're a detective, aren't you? Detect. Good day." With that, the man continued down the hill, stopping at the bottom to doff his top hat before disappearing.

Putting on his favourite mocking voice, Harry mimicked. "You're a detective, aren't you? Detect." He ripped open the plastic wrapping and snapped the biscuit in half, finding another folded piece of paper baked into it. "If this was Scooby Doo, my money would be on him. With luck, I'll get to rip his face off later." Folding open the note, Harry read the next instalment as an ambulance siren wailed in the distance.

23 August 1682

After a few days finding the ingredients necessary to quell the waking spirits of this land, I decided it best to infiltrate the nearby village of Clagton, the place which has threatened everything that my forebears and I had worked so hard to maintain.

For nigh on a week I posed as a wishing well, doing little more than arrange a number of clay bricks around my feet, hold a broken branch in my hands, and rest a rusting bucket upon my head. For seven days and nights I stood there, soaking in all the prejudices and simple ways that the village folk hold within their crooked hearts.

I discovered a number of things. First, every man-jack of them is blessed with minimal intelligence. Not one questioned how a wishing well had materialised in their midst —overnight. By the end of the week, so complete was my acceptance that many locals rested upon my knee. After telling me about their daily malaise or a morsel of gossip about the lust they held for their cousin, they would cast a shiny sixpence into the small corral of bricks before going about their business. By the end of my stint there, I had amassed enough coin to buy another cat, and many rare herbs which I would have otherwise been unable to obtain.

Second, their distrust of the supernatural does not lie solely at my door. I heard many a villager tell another things they claimed to have seen, but which were utterly fabricated. The tales ranged from people turning into pieces of furniture to lumbering landmarks that had made off with their first-born in the night. I do admit to a pang of guilt after snatching seven newborns one evening, but my constitution was suffering and only the blood and flesh of the innocent would allow me to maintain my subterfuge.

Having returned to my lodge, I am sated in the knowledge that although they possess violence which can be summoned with little more than a change in wind direction, they could be easily distracted. I shall use this information to my advantage in future encounters. Of that I have no doubt.

"Can we take him now, sir?" The paramedic asked again, this time tapping a wristwatch.

"Yeah, why not. In fact, you can give me a lift back to the hospital while you're at it," Harry replied, folding the paper up and tucking it into his swimming trunks.

With the ambulance's back doors open, the paramedics exchanged a look before wheeling the stricken Wonky Tab inside. Harry held out a hand. "Hold up, best get this inside first." The detective dragged his trebuchet across to the back of the ambulance, grabbed hold of one end and nodded towards the other side. "Well?"

"Well what?" The medics replied in unison, peas from the same pod, so attuned that they did practically everything together.

"Can one of you knobbers help me get this in the back? It's heavier than it looks, you know."

Shaking his head, the wristwatch paramedic laughed before falling silent. "You're...you're serious?"

"As a fucking heart attack."

"But what about him?" The medic pointed to Wonky, who was tucked up beneath a smashing red blanket and strapped into the stretcher lest any comedy moments happen to him should he be accidentally tipped out.

Harry sized the gurney and man combo up. "We can squidge him in after. Come on, get a wriggle on."

Chapter
Five

Gypsophila paniculata

Jan checked that the door number hadn't slipped upside down, and that number 36 was actually that, not 39. That might explain why no-one was answering the door; the other possibility was that it was those pesky kids again. "Pesky kids," she grumbled under her breath, to emphasise the point that it could be those pesky kids. Again.

Reaching into her coat pocket, she rummaged through the assortment of items in there, ignoring the brass knuckle-dusters, Afghan hound puppy and collapsible satellite dish. Instead, she pulled out her spare door knocker and rapped it against the door with as much might as she could muster, without endangering the hinges and being wanted for breaking and entering.

In her defence —and it's one she'd use in a court of law— with the door to that last house being knocked down, the law could be interpreted that she had been invited in. To that end, what some people (namely the homeowner and police) would call burglary, she would argue was called a "long term lend." She'd get her turn in the dock; she wasn't fussed.

Just as she was about to piss in the flowerbed, she heard a key turn in the lock. A crack appeared between door and jamb, and a man's sweaty face appeared. "Yes? Hello?"

"You ordered a special delivery?" Jan asked, waving the item gently, hoping it would jog the simpleton's memory.

"Ah yes. Of course. Thank you for coming so promptly, I need these, I can tell you. Ha." The laugh was a hollow one, filled with nothing of substance, like a budget chocolate éclair filled with powdery cream barely fit for human consumption. The door swung open to reveal the man standing there, naked except for an apron which was wound tightly around his midriff. The cord was biting into his skin, pushing squishy mounds of dimpled flesh to bulge up either side of the string.

Jan suppressed a guffaw with the back of her hand and held out the delivery in the other. "Here you go, Mr…Smith…this should iron out any kinks you may be experiencing."

Mr…Smith was reaching for the object when the subtle meaning of the woman's words hit home. He went red from head to toe, except where the tie-string was cutting off circulation. "Erm…thanks." Taking the bunch of flowers from Jan, his nose started to twitch. "Mmm, what is that smell? It's like a rubber spanking paddle."

This was enough to send Jan over the edge of chuckle mountain, and despite every attempt at maintaining professionalism, she couldn't help but dangle from laughing peak.

"What?" Having replayed the words in his mind, Mr…Smith went redder still, his skin adopting the same tone as Sonny the sunburnt beetroot who was the face of the Dulux 'Red Range' advertising campaign in 1987. "I meant…that's an odd smell for a bouquet. Please tell me, why does it smell like that and not like a summer meadow?"

Jan shrugged, pulled out the first of a string of magician tissues from her pocket —which looked like a length of bunting— and blew her nose. "Sorry, I can't smell a thing at the moment, got this blooming cold."

"Oh. Well, in that case, you aren't aware of the aroma of this particular flower. I must say, it looks very unusual."

"They're special, locally-grown don't you know? Only had them in this morning, it was the strangest thing …"

"They do smell like a rubber paddle, you know, the kind you use to gently thwack against—" Mr…Smith's mouth stayed open, unable to fathom having been thrown under the proverbial bus by his brain once more.

This was enough for Jan. She swivelled on the gravel path and headed back to her van, waving off the grunting and gentle sobs from the apron-clad man. As she got to the car, she chanced one final peek, only to see Mr…Smith turn and talk to someone unseen within the house, inadvertently baring his naked plum-coloured buttocks to the woman who realised that the drive back to her florist would be dicey, given the sights and information she had been privy to over the last few minutes.

"Was that *her*?" A woman's voice shouted down the hallway from the kitchen.

With the door closed, and the sound of a van engine gunning to life, Vince tugged down on the apron, looked towards the artex ceiling and counted to ten before replying. Managing to get to six before the question was repeated, this time loud enough to shake the letterbox cover, he replied back with his sweetest voice. "No, my love, of course not."

"Then who was it? I definitely heard a woman's voice."

"It was, but—"

"So it was *her* then? How dare you talk to her when I told you not to. No. Didn't *tell* you not to, I *commanded* you not to. Stack up the washing, it's gone frothy. My mother was right about you."

"Honestly, my love. It wasn't *her*."

"Then who was it? Tell you what. Examine the small print. Don't answer me out there, when you can stick your fingers up at me, text her, or write a little love letter. Get your useless sack of shit arse in here. Podgy dumplings."

Vince sagged, hid the flowers behind his back and trudged down the hallway, his slippers patting softly against the polished wooden floorboards. The kitchen stretched the width of the back of the house, the dining room to one side. Taking up most of the space in the room was a large oak table. Bar the head of the table, five chunky matching chairs were pushed in, ready for any guests or unannounced visitors. Vince stuck his head round the doorway. "I've got you a surprise."

"Shut your stupid mouth, Vincent. Get in here properly, so I can see you. I need to behead you for lapping up my cereal milk. Gone bad, Muncher, it has."

Still holding the flowers behind him, Vince stepped into the room, head bowed, and made his way to the table. "Here I am, my love."

"Don't you, *my love* me, you useless bastard. What were you doing out there? Who was at the door? Why were they here? Is that the latest episode of my favourite show on the telly? Muncher."

Vince looked across the oaken expanse of table at his wife, who was placed at the head of it. This was apt, because her head was all that was left of her.

In a large circular fishbowl floated the noggin of his deceased wife, Veronica. The decomposing skull bobbed within, eyes long since rolled upwards, only the gone-off white sclera showing. Her mouth was agape, transfixed in her final moment of surprise, as the Christmas tree box had caught her square in the ribcage, inadvertently mirroring the four-finger death-punch made famous by Buddhist monks who had sworn off religious servitude and turned to breath-taking violence instead.

"It was just a delivery lady. Here, these are for you," Vince pulled out the flowers with a flourish, even going so far as to add a, "da-dah," into the mix. Classy. But let's face it, we all do it from time to time.

"Lumpy catfish spit. Makes me look at everyone," came the reply. Veronica's head listed slightly within the gloop her husband had concocted to stave off the ravages of decomposition.

Vince set the flowers down on the table and scuttled across to his wife's decapitated skull. Set either side of the fishbowl were two speakers, the cables trailing across the floor to a laptop, set on the largest table from a nest. Unlocking the screen, Vince pored over the display. "Something's not right with the coding…too many anomalies getting in. Hope it's not the beginning of another cascade failure."

"Polish your nuts. Vincent. You waste of rubbish tin cans. Spank me on my fringe. Mincemeat poker, Muncher."

He tapped away on the keyboard, trying to isolate the issue. He hit *Enter* and stood up. Pulling out a modified remote control from the apron pocket, he turned the dial so it went from 'nasty and controlling' to 'grateful and sweet'.

Clearing his throat, he tried again. "Hi, sweetie. I got you a surprise."

The speakers crackled into life. "Aww, for me? Honey, thank you so much."

"They're your favourites, too."

"Aww, thank you. What are they?"

Vince picked up the bunch of flowers and tried to remember what he'd ordered. "Erm…they're posies."

"Posies? They *are* my favourite. You're my favourite little bucket of spunk gobbling arse loving muncher. Muncher. Muncher. MUNCHER MUNCHER MUNCHER MUNCHER"

"Not again, you're in a feedback loop, my love."

"MUNCHER MUNCHER MUNCHER MUNCHER MUNCHER"

Vince pressed the power button on the speakers and sighed as the last "MUNCHER," faded into nothingness. Kneeling down so that his eyeline was level with the vacant stare of his wife, he stroked the side of the glass. "Don't worry, I'll iron the bugs out. You'll be back up and running in no time at all. Perhaps next time you can order me round some more…I've been a very naughty boy."

From the end of the table came that smell again. Before he even knew it, Vince had picked up the flowers and was standing over the peculiar technological setup, fashioned so he could keep his soulmate alive in the only way he knew how.

Weirdly.

But with limited science.

"Look how beautiful they are …" Vince held the flowers out to the floating head, even though the only thing Veronica's eyes could see —if they were still plugged into a nervous system that was operational— was the inside of her slowly rotting skull, "… just like you."

Unable to refrain any longer, Vince held the bunch of flowers to his face and took a deep breath in. Amongst the posies (for real) and other regular flowers sat one that you are becoming familiar with. It closed around the bottom of his face, accommodating the man's beard, and went to work in rendering the human unconscious.

Vince collapsed forward, sending the bouquet into the bowl of head and homemade embalming fluid. It wasn't a good mix; the flowers began to curl up and wither. Smacking into the table, Vince bounced off the speaker, the power button flickering on as he fell backwards, landing in a crumpled pile of red flesh on the floor.

A mournful voice bellowed out of the speaker. "MUNCHER MUNCHER-"

Chapter
Six

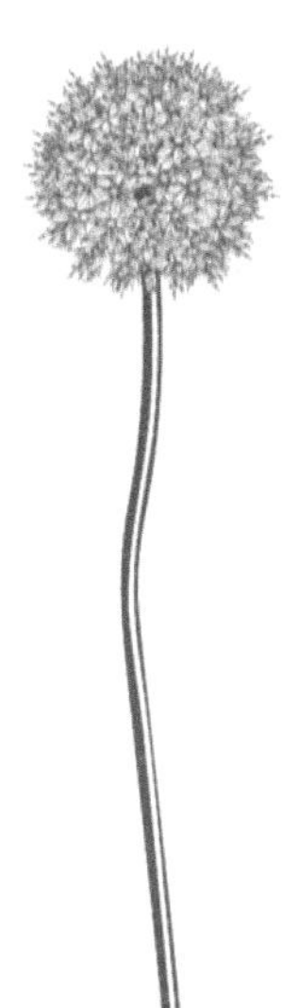

Allium giganteum

A Few Moments Earlier…

Harry leaned over the shoulder of the ambulance driver, who shall be referred to as 'Tanner' in the upcoming dialogue sections. "Go on, you know you want to."

Tanner shied away from the man, eyes fixed to the road. "No. There's no need to."

"Go on."

"No."

"Just a little bit."

"I can't, it's not allowed."

The detective edged closer, whispering into Tanner's ear. "Telling me it's against the rules just makes me want to do it even more."

"I don't care. I'm not doing it, there is no chance in hell."

"What do you reckon, Burned-and-Crispy?" Harry shouted to the paramedic in the rear of the ambulance, sandwiched snugly between unconscious patient on the stretcher and the trebuchet. Quite why Harry had decided on that nickname for the poor medic was anyone's guess. Burned-and-Crispy tried to shake his head but realised that one wrong move could set the weapon off, which could cost him an ear, or worse. "No. We'd be crucified as an offering to appease the ambulance gods if we did."

"You guys are no fun." Harry scanned the dashboard and the rows and rows of buttons and switches. "If you don't, I'll just start button-mashing." This did little to provoke a positive response, so Harry chose the closest button to him —a red one in the shape of The Star of David, and smacked it with the palm of his hand. "KABLAM!"

"Noooooooooooo." Tanner shouted in slow motion, even though time was running at normal speed. If anything, time was running slightly faster than normal; experts estimate around 1.05% more rapidly, in fact. And whilst that doesn't sound much, if you multiply that out, it can mean losing around three seconds every half hour.

There was a WUMPH sound from the rear of the vehicle, coupled with a shriek. Harry glanced in the rear-view mirror in time to see Burned-and-Crispy get ejected out of the ambulance sunroof. Nothing too odd in that, except his left buttock was on fire. The scream faded away as the hapless paramedic arced over the front of the cab, landing on a petrol station forecourt like a friendly fire mortar.

As the ambulance drove past, and despite having broken a leg and being in possession of a singed arse cheek, Burned-and-Crispy gave a thumbs up. "Hey, you carry on, I'll be fine from—" He never got the chance to finish his sentence, as his fiery thumb lit up a cloud of petrol fumes, setting in motion an explosive chain reaction which took out everything in a half-mile radius, and which was visible from my back garden.

I understand now why Harry named him so.

Harry slumped in the passenger seat and glared at Tanner. "Nice one, prick stain."

"How is that my fault?"

"All I wanted you to do was turn the siren on, and *now* look. People are dead, dying and on fire. This is going to go in my report, you know, and…spoiler alert, you don't come out of it with flying colours."

Tanner wrestled with the steering wheel as the aftershock threatened to tip the ambulance over, which would leave it at the mercy of the slowly pouring lava, which had erupted from the sundered earth. (Come on, you must know that all petrol stations are built on volcanoes? No? You ever tried reading proper books? You know, about actual real-life things? You should do, I read them all the time. I even get the audiobooks when I'm writing just so I can learn things like this.)

Snapping the wheel to one side, the ambulance was back on four wheels, and after wiping his sweaty brow, Tanner shook his head. "Rules are rules, given the patient's condition and the amount of traffic on the roads, we just don't need to put the siren on. The lights are more than enough, if anything, even *they* are overkill."

"Pussy." Harry used the cover of his sunglasses to make it look like he was staring at the driver, whilst really, his eyes were scanning the console.

"SOK!" His hand shot out and flipped a chunky switch shaped like an antique bottle of lemonade.

The bonnet split in two and opened up like a pair of hands gesturing 'book' in the classic game *Charades,* often deployed at Christmas family parties when people are too pissed and/or apathetic to converse anymore.

A geriatric strip-a-gram appeared out of the engine bay, with only duct tape saving bits and pieces from the cruel grip of droopage. Unfortunately, her atrophied limbs —she had been in there for some time— and duct tape did little to arrest gravity slamming her from the only home she had ever known and up against the windscreen. As Harry gazed into the hairy hinterland of Phyllis Sux, he reconsidered his life choices. "Okay, fine, I don't need the siren. Just please…send the ancient saggy stripper on her way." The duct tape around Phyllis' pelvic area began to peel off, the end flapping in the air as the ambulance continued at a steady forty miles an hour. "Quickly now, I'm in danger of staring into the Eye of Sauron if any more tape comes off."

"Hang on," Tanner replied.

Reaching by the side of the steering wheel, he pulled a plastic arm up and the windscreen wipers kicked into life. They pushed and squeezed the old woman's skeletal form against the window. Every backward swipe snagged on decrepit skin, rolling it out like cracked, dry pastry.

"It's not working," Harry muttered, wanting to look away but utterly entranced by the greying pelvic thicket being smeared against the glass in front of him.

Tanner yanked the arm up, increasing the motor speed of the wiper blades. After a few awkward seconds, there was a sonic boom, and the craggy stripper was hurled from the windscreen and into a passing carnival attraction, hitting a singular coconut and winning a teddy bear laced with strychnine for her troubles. "Happy now?"

"Much better, are we there yet?"

"Nearly, hold on to something." Tanner wrenched the steering wheel and the tyres screeched in complaint. Slamming on the brakes, the ambulance came to a stop under a covered bay. The paramedic turned the engine off and sat there for a moment, his head in his hands.

Harry reached out and patted the man on the back.

"DON'T TOUCH ME!" Tanner screamed, making the detective press up against his window. Lifting his head, the driver turned slowly to look at his tormentor. "I'm going to go now. I never want to see you again."

"Fair enough, I-"

The ice-pick was out of Tanner's pocket and against Harry's throat in a flash. "I bloody well mean it. If I see you again…I'm going to stick you. I know things. Bad things. Places I could jab you with this that no one will be able to stitch up. You'll die slowly, all the while hallucinating that you're a figment of your own imagination."

With the tip pressing into his flesh, Harry mumbled a "yes," in hope that the peril would pass. Tanner closed his eyes, lost in a memory of paramedic training camp where they'd all learned how to mess people up with different implements. Snapping out of it, he opened the door, and slammed it shut.

-MUNCHER MUNCHER-

Sorry, that seeped in from the previous chapter.

Tenderly dabbing his throat, Harry checked that the man was out of earshot before whispering, "Touchy." He decided mentally that he'd count to ten —which comes directly after nine— then get out and see if Dr. Singh had metaphorically pulled finger from arse and made some actual progress. Getting up to eight-and-three-quarters, he heard a scrabbling sound come from the glove compartment. After a quick check to make sure it wasn't the grumpy driver, Harry pulled on the handle.

Barnaby's head and shoulders bulged from the small compartment. His head was hatless, which struck Harry as the oddest thing. "Good day, detective, fare thee well?"

"I've had better days, if I'm being truthful."

"Haven't we all? Though for some, this day is becoming quite the trial." Barnaby twisted and turned his head, all the while maintaining eye contact. This served to free his right arm from the confines of the plastic space.

"How did…" Harry began, then realised that all you get in response to a stupid question …

"Find the sword at the bottom of the ocean, with only your wits," Barnaby jabbered.

"Huh?"

"A stupid answer. It's what you get if you ask a stupid question."

"How did…"

"…"

Harry held his hand over Barnaby's mouth. "No, I don't want to know. Just tell me what you're here for, this is getting tedious."

Barnaby's eyes rolled down to the hand clamped over his noise-hole. Harry took the hint and pulled it away, gratefully noting that he wasn't covered in spittle. "I think you'll be needing this, good sir." Barnaby's one free hand shoved another plastic-wrapped biscuit – a ginger nut – under Harry's nose.

"Fuck the Pope in the stinkhole, another one?"

"Oh yes, I fear there will be many more before this day is through."

"Any chance of helping me?"

Looking a tad hurt, Barnaby replied, "What do you think I'm doing? Are these biscuit crumbs not helping?"

"This is the third one, not exactly illuminating at the moment, are they?"

"They get better, I promise. Plus, I think with this and the information from the last one, you will have some clues to follow up on, hmm?"

Harry snatched the biscuit from the strange man. "This is all terribly fucking convenient, you know. *Too* convenient if you ask me."

Barnaby shrugged with one shoulder, a strange motion to be sure. "Until we meet again. Which may be sooner than you think …" He wriggled within the plastic prison, which squeaked in annoyance. His face began to bubble, the skin pulsing and rippling.

"Are you okay there?" Harry asked.

With his eyes darting from side-to-side, Barnaby beckoned the detective closer with a twitch of his moustache. "Would you mind terribly if you…sodded off? Just I'm having a little trouble getting out of here and it's going to ruin the majesty of my future appearances if you see me like this for too long."

"Shall I just?" Harry thumbed to the passenger door.

"If you don't mind? That would be super."

Harry pushed his sunglasses up the bridge of his nose. "Sure thing. See you later, you fucking weirdo."

"Bye. Bye-bye."

25 August 1682

I have been back in my lodge for two days now, and ever since I set foot on the leaf mulch flooring, I have been plagued by a nagging doubt. Spurning the embrace of slumber, I have spent that time trying to work out the cause of my uncertainty. It is only now that I realise it is not one thing, but a great many.

My cauldrons have been re-smelted; divots and scratches no longer adorn the surfaces which are now smooth and true. My original black cat —Knight, the one I have had since mother taught me my first curse— was behaving oddly. It was only when I discovered an egg in her snoozing basket that I discovered she was in fact a chicken. Two false legs had been fashioned from wooden cutlery and affixed to the breast, in addition to a long tail, made of knitted wool hanging from its rear, and it was painted comb-to-claw in tar. Where has my precious Knight been spirited away to?

My ingredients, key to not just my survival but to placating the fey spirits of this dell, have been exchanged for common twigs and moss, lichen and grass, which will serve no purpose other than to enrage both the phantoms and I. The mattress upon which I lay each night, an extravagance I allowed myself when mother was tried and executed, now rested on a bed that listed to one side. On closer inspection, a book, detailing neighbouring counties and their various covens, propped up one leg.

It was then I discovered the biggest act of sabotage. Every branch and leaf that had been used to build my lodge turned out to be nothing but stale loaves. Long baguettes replaced load-bearing branches, whilst individual slices of bread acted as roof tiles, covering my abode. With autumn around the corner I knew they would not be able to keep the rain and inclement weather from dampening my possessions and body.

It was then that it hit me. The Clagton villagers I had pegged for fools, had instead fooled me. That week when I thought I was observing them was turned on its head; my belongings ransacked and swapped out, the lodge my ancestors had built with their own hands transformed into little more than a poor gingerbread man's house.

To what end, I knew not. As I stroked chicken-Knight — his tacky feathers a poor substitute for real cat fur— I understood what they wanted. They wanted me out. It was so clear now. Fine. If that was their intention, who am I to disappoint? Though this land will be much changed when I leave, and those damn villagers, thinking themselves above me in both intellect and faith, will discover the true extent of my powers.

"Ooh, it's getting interesting now," Dr. Singh cooed over Harry's shoulder.

Shrugging the man away, Harry squared up to him. "What have I told you? This is evidence in an ongoing case, you shouldn't be reading it. Besides, what are you doing out here?"

A squall of sirens broke the silence deadlock. Singh pointed to the driveway as an ambulance skidded around the corner at speed. "We've had another call come in; you know, flower-related. Man found in his house, near-naked, too, nothing but an apron tightly wound around his waist. Ha, you should hear what they found in there. His dead wife's head in a jar, and a laptop trying to vocally emulate different aspects of her personality. Only reason we found him was that the neighbours called the cops because of the noise."

"What noise? Something different about him, was there?"

"Oh no, nothing like that. He's out for the count, like the other two. Flower over his nose, comatose, being kept alive. We've got a specialist coming in from Basingstoke. Big hotshot flower expert by all accounts, she'll know what's going on —you mark my words. No, the neighbours kept hearing *muncher* being shouted over and over again. First off, they thought they could be referring to the main location for their upcoming German trip, well, before the wife passed, but no. It was the speakers going mental."

"Cool story."

"Really?"

"No, it's fucking shit. So this is victim number three?" Harry counted off on his fingers.

"It is. Wonder how many more we'll get?"

Harry flashed off his watch. "The day is still young. I've got a feeling we're far from through the worst of it."

The ambulance crashed into the back of the one ahead of it, sending shards of glass in a wide arc; pieces of broken bumper and bent metal lay on the floor from the impact. The driver of the new arrival fell out of the cab, before gingerly picking himself up. Stumbling to the rear, rubbing his neck, he knew he'd be hauled in front of another disciplinary hearing. The crash was one thing but using the sirens in a non-essential call was tantamount to medical heresy.

"Do you think they'll mind if I borrow their wheels?" Harry pointed to the ambulance he'd arrived in. "Just my trebuchet in the back —and it was a complete bastard to get in there, be worse now with the back end all smashed in."

Dr. Singh was breathing on his stethoscope, heading towards the new passenger being extricated from the crashed ambulance. "Go for it, if it still works."

Harry opened the door and got in, seeing that Barnaby had extricated himself from the glove box and the keys had been left in the ignition. He gunned the engine and grinned the grin of victory (+10 to Persuade). "Works like a charm," he said, slamming the door shut and reaching across to the endless bank of buttons, hoping to strike it lucky with the siren and lights.

"Hey, where are you going? You know, in case there are any developments I need to tell you about." Singh called out, checking Vince's vital signs and the apron's pattern: black-and-white stripes. Nice. A timeless classic.

After deploying an emergency dinghy, firing out a homing missile destined for the local moonshine still, and changing the primary colour of the vehicle from white to turquoise, he finally found the switch he was looking for. The siren screamed into life, a disco ball popped out of the roof, and the blue lights kicked in. Making sure his sunglasses were straight, Harry replied, "Where else would anyone go to get information?"

"The internet? On your phone?"

Harry shook his head. "Don't have one, just my trusty pager."

"Why not?" Singh pressed his thumb into Vince's rectum for no other reason than he was stalling for time and he liked doing it.

The detective pointed to the heavens. "Aliens. Nope, I'm off to the library. There's an old friend down there who can help me piece this clusterfuck together. Toodles." Cranking the siren volume up to brain-cell-killing levels, Harry pressed down on the accelerator, saluted, and lurched out of the A&E delivery bay.

Chapter
Seven

Astilbe biternata

Around three miles down the road from the centre of Charlton village, the library in Andover town centre was a relic from the sixties. Built in the middle of the town, the repository of books and arcane knowledge had suffered the indignity of having a shopping centre built around it in the late eighties. Now, after people had decided what book to borrow, they could leave and walk into the supermarket opposite, thus completing two essential chores relatively painlessly.

Harry had ditched the now-smouldering ambulance in a bus bay and was striding past the shops, eager to get his hands on something, anything, which might shed some light on the events of the day. Mothers and fathers shielded their children's eyes from the sight of the man walking past them, still dressed in nothing but his blue speedos, sunglasses, and jaunty smirk.

Pushing through the library doors, Harry took a final drag on the cigarette before passing the near-spent butt to a homeless beagle, who took it gladly. In another odd design decision, the library itself was spread across the first floor, accessible only via a flight of stairs or an elevator which had been known to completely ignore the button presses and transport any person it deemed unworthy of the library's knowledge down into the basement, straight into the incinerator.

Sure, the local paper's letters section was filled with complaints about its nature, but the council decided to let it be. That elevator had replaced another one, which had a penchant for squashing down anyone who failed to say please when deciding on the floor they wished to be deposited to. Harsh, but fair. Manners maketh the elevator, that's what mummy always said.

Harry took the stairs two at a time, arriving at the top a little out of breath, but un-conflagrated, which was important if he were to continue with his investigation. Death would've voided his temporary employment, and it would fall to someone else to pick up the mantle. Given the hours elapsed and the clues dispersed already, they'd have to be a savant to get up to speed in the time they had left to avoid impending floral disaster.

I've said too much.

The receptionist raised her one good eye at the man, then pointed to the back of the library. "He's over there. Organising the back catalogues of Playboy and Razzle."

Little natural light filtered into the building; the windows that were exposed to the outside world and not the murk of the shopping centre had tall established trees in bloom in front of them. Added to the muck and grime that accumulated there from the late-night drag racing strip that ran from the Guildhall opposite, it was a wonder the employees didn't sue for Vitamin E deficiencies.

The lighting cast a pallid glow as Harry worked his way down past the sections on doughnut making, black hole conjuring and reptilian housebreaking, before three more steps up took him to the reference section at the back of the floor. There, true to the receptionist's word, was the hulking robot, BU-4T, which Harry had come to see.

Approaching the machine, the small dish and antenna assembly on its head pointed in Harry's direction. As its multiple mechanical hands sorted at speed, each ending in a wide blunt pincer, the robot turned to face its visitor. Its head was like those of most automatons, with round eyes which lit from within like fading car headlights. Its nose was nothing more than an intake port which BU-4T used to sample the atmosphere around him. In mere seconds, it could determine who had dropped a fart in the library elevator. The mouth was a large rectangular grille with a screen behind it, which crackled when it bothered to speak, as it would do now. "It's you," it growled, any inflection lost in its vocal processors, which made it sound like it smoked cigars all day long and gargled on motor oil.

"BU, old friend, how's it going?"

Stopping its sorting, the machine rolled across to the now-stationary detective, coming to an awkward halt on its twin motorised tracks. At nine-foot tall, it easily loomed over the humanoid. "Illogical. Does not compute." Each of its ten arms were outstretched, pincers open wide.

"I've come down here to speak of Ollopi-Prime Delta."

At this, the robot's eye lights changed from vanilla to strawberry in colour. The pincers folded back in on themselves, and from hidden ports came weapons of every kind. There was a flamethrower —pretty standard—and an electrical fork which had arcs of lightning jumping from one tendril to the other, purely for effect. Plus the whole gamut of projectile weapons, missile launchers, spikes, blades, you name a weapon and you can bet your non-metal arse it was now sticking out of BU-4T's limbs and pointing at Harry. "We do not speak of that day."

The detective pulled off his sunglasses. "Bullshit, we'll speak of it if I want to. Who saved you? Huh? Yeah, that's right, bitch, me. After your little escape pod jettisoned that dead world and crash-landed here, who managed to get every single one of your wheels rolling again? Who panel-beat every dent out of your chassis? Who…who taught you how to love?"

BU-4T let off a series of clicks and whirrs as its mini-gun revved up to speed to help with the delivery of high-calibre rounds which would disintegrate the meat-man in front of it. "You did all of those things. Except for the last thing. I am not organic; I am incapable of…love."

"You're damn right, love is for wusses. But who disabled your ability to harm another living person? Huh?"

Try as he might —and he bloody well tried, believe me— BU-4T could not trigger any of his weapons. Each internal request met with a negative response. Harry hooked the arm of his sunglasses over the rail gun and pulled down, the limb falling limply with it. "See. You think I'd put back together the greatest killing machine in the entire galaxy and let it go BOOM-BOOM whenever it wanted? Pah! You must think me some kind of idiot."

"I do. But regrettably I am unable to terminate your life-force with extreme prejudice." One by one, the weapon systems flicked off, the arms retracting telescopically back into the main arms, which then hung loosely by BU's side.

"Plus, who's your number one guy that got you this sweet gig? Huh? Huh?" Harry flicked his shades out and put them back on, arms out wide, taking in the full spectrum of books, magazines and outdated storage medium that were on display.

"This is no…sweet gig…as you would say. I spend my days sorting through the detritus of your pathetic civilisation, learning of your predilections and weaknesses. The only thing stopping me from self-destructing is that I may use this information one day to help me take over this puny planet."

"The only thing?"

"Fine. That, and the fact that you have my self-destruction firing pin."

"And don't you fucking forget it. Now, before we get back to business, I'm feeling a bit glum, so I want you to do *the thing*."

"Why do you always seek to demean me in this way?"

"Because it cheers me up, and I built it in when I repaired you. Now, you can do it voluntarily, or I can just say the command and you'll do it anyway, up to you, BU."

"I refuse to agr-"

"Initiate stored procedure, SP_TURN_INTO_A-"

"Fine." BU-4T collapsed his arms into his chassis, which disappeared behind sliding metal panels. Tottering from side-to-side, he slowly built up momentum, leaning further over with every rock. Just at the point where he fell over, the machine mournfully intoned. "Down I go."

Demolishing an antique table which was used solely for putting tired feet onto, and displaying the decorative flags from domesticated underwater worlds, BU-4T laid on its side, its twin tracks buzzing round in the air. Harry fell to the floor, clutching his sides, laughing so loudly that the books on nearby shelves were trying to shush him. "Help me. Help me. I am just a stupid, lame robot," BU added.

"You are, you are," Harry bellowed, his stomach aching from hearty laughter.

"Am I done now?"

The detective shook his head. "Oh no, you know what you have to do to finish it off."

Sighing, BU-4T opened up a small square panel on the front of his body, around where his groin would be if we were to humanise him. Harry pushed himself to his knees, trying to suppress the inevitable hilarity that was about to befall him. The robot discharged a stream of steaming oil from the revealed hole, spraying the remnants of the table. Harry fell onto his back, on the verge of pissing himself. "Say the words," he shouted.

"Oh no, I've had a trouser accident. Please help me. I am just a stupid lame robot who cannot control his bladder."

"You mucky pup, I can't take you anywhere." Harry removed his sunglasses and dabbed at his tear-heavy eyes with pieces of torn magazine pages and scraps of flag cloth.

"Can I stand now and resume my servitude?"

"Yeah, go on, though I do have some questions for you."

A metal pin ejected from the robot's shoulder, pressing into the ground and lifting him back to his full vertical height. "It is an illogical request to ask of me. I don't even have a bladder."

"I know."

"Then why do you insist I say the words?"

"Because it's funny. Fucking hell, don't you be getting all touchy, you metal prick. You grown a vagina since I last saw you? Ordered one from Metal Dickheads Dot Com?"

"No such website exists."

Harry stood up and jabbed a finger under the robot's grille. "Shut the fuck up, or I'll have you crushed down for scrap, you hear me? Piece of shit has forgotten who saved who."

BU-4T stood immobile, his eye lights pulsing gently as his central processor seethed inside. A killing machine like this shouldn't have to take such nonsense from an organism that it would ordinarily have turned into fertiliser before destroying its home. The number of planets it had laid low. Admittedly, most of which were razed because it had powered up on the wrong side of the charging bay. A number of civilisations had been exterminated simply because BU-4T had not had its morning dump of overnight bug reports to its archive folder.

"Good. Now, I need some information, quick sharp. A number of people have been incapacitated by a strange flower."

The machine's eyes glowed brightly, its mouth grille crackling with life. "That sounds…unfortunate."

"You bet your tiny metal knob it is. Some nonce has been giving me pieces of the puzzle, and I need to get to the bottom of it, pronto. I've got a quiz down the Rogering Ram tonight, there is no way I'm missing it. First prize is a month's supply of steak, and it's got my name on it."

"If it has your name on it, why do you need to win it? Can you just not acquire the object as it is clearly marked as your property?"

Harry kicked the robot, though with no shoes on, all he managed was a broken little toe. "It's a saying, pissypants. Look, do me a favour and let me tell you what I need. Then you do what you do, give me the information and I'll be out of your wiry pubes, deal?"

BU-4T remained motionless.

"Good. Now, the diary notes mention Clagton…I need to find out where that is, it's not anywhere nearby, that's for sure —otherwise I'd have heard of it."

"There are a number of books in this section which can assist you in this matter."

Harry slapped the robot's head. "Listen here, static-breath, reading books is for losers. I'm no loser, I'm a majestic winner. If I wanted to read the book that told me the answer to my question, I'd be a speccy-faced loser who can't find anyone to have sex with. You know what books is short for, don't you?"

"Books is not a shortened word, it—"

"Zip it, Wi-Fi head. Books is short for bollocks. So, unless you have the answer for me in a movie adaptation —ideally with Helen Mirren and/or Morgan Freeman— then I ain't interested. Either rustle up the information in the next ten seconds, or I'm going to reprogram you so that the only job you can get is fellating exhaust pipes."

BU-4T's lights shimmered, before the wheeled tracks down one side spun into life and the machine ground over the debris from his earlier fall. Coming to a stop in front of the sole microfiche unit in Andover, he snaked a cable out from one of his arms and slid it into the machine. After some whirring and clunks, BU said, "Here."

Harry run his finger across the screen, his lips moving as he read. "No way…Charlton used to be called Clagton. Kinda makes sense now."

"UNAUTHORISED PRESENCE DETECTED IN CENTRAL BAY," BU bellowed, a klaxon blaring for dramatic effect.

"What's got into you?"

On cue, the front of the robot's body fell open, and Barnaby bid welcome with the obligatory tip of his hat. "Ah, my dear boy, it appears you are finally on the trail, joyous news indeed. However …" The man coughed, his eyes shifting sideways to an outstretched hand, clasping an oversized pink wafer wrapped in plastic.

"You mean?"

Barnaby simpered. "I'm afraid so, old bean, there's been another *incident*."

"But I would know about it if there had been, or someone would have had the detail recounted to them in third person, surely?" Harry glowered at BU-4T who stood in stoic silence.

"Not so, chum. One can only go over the events so many times before it loses some of its impact. No, three times is plenty for one person to get the general gist, from now on in it'll only be key personnel that we'll go into the minutiae with."

"That's something I can get behind. I bet you're still going to appear in random places, aren't you?"

"You betcha. As I said from the beginning, I am here to help guide you through these testing times. I fear without my assistance you and your fellow authoritarian figures would be none the wiser."

"I'd argue that we're still none the fucking wiser."

Barnaby pulled himself out of the robot's body, careful to not pull on any important wires or accidentally let off any ordinance. "Tish and pish. I would counter that if you pulled your finger out a little sooner, then you would be well on the road to discovering the cause of this little problem. Now, I bid you good day."

The detective watched as the man strode out of sight, rapping his cane on the brim of his hat as he disappeared. "In the competition of prize cocks, that man takes the whole winner's trophy right up the shitpipe."

"UNAUTHORISED PRESENCE DETECTED IN CENTRAL BAY," BU-4T bellowed once more, the annoying klaxon punctuating the sentence.

"What the? —" Harry turned back to the robot, who had still to close the panel from before.

There, in the chasm once more, was Barnaby, who doffed his hat. "Good day, detective. I have something further for you."

As the man passed Harry a sealed hazelnut and (milk) chocolate chip cookie, Harry shook his head. "Another one? So soon? This is taking the piss."

"Bear with me one moment," Barnaby replied. His other hand disappeared into the machine's innards, appearing with a large sealed Jaffa Cake. "This one too. I'm guessing it was twins."

"Is a Jaffa Cake a biscuit?"

"Well, technically, no, but it's still available down the biscuit aisle so I'm allowing it."

"At this rate, my BMI is going to be fucked."

"You're not eating them, are you?"

"Well yeah, what else am I supposed to do, use them as incontinence pads? Besides, do you see pockets on my current ensemble?"

Barnaby had extricated himself again from the robot. He repeated his leaving process and, well, left.

"What a bellend." Harry snapped open the pink wafer biscuit, smelling one half before shoving it in his gob.

27 August 1682

It has taken me two days to venture forth into the darkest depths of the dell and return to my home. I was able to identify my lodge before I could even see it, as the smell of mouldy bread carried well on the stern breeze. My quest was not in vain.

Using my ancestor's diary, I was able to identify a unique strain of flower which will assist me in getting my revenge on those retched villagers.

"Finally, we're fucking getting somewhere."

Found in only one place, by the banks of the foul cursed swamp, I was able to bring back a near perfect specimen. All I need now is to read some more of mother's spell books, perhaps volume three of the Greater Spell Series—

"I knew it, a bloody bollock reader."

—which contains something I can use to enhance its already potent powers. This entry will be brief, for I need to prepare, and with my tools replaced with inferior ware, I

need to source alternatives.

Harry finished the other half of the biscuit before unwrapping the Jaffa Cake. "This is all well and good, but the name of the village isn't much to go on." This sheet of paper was near blank, save for a scribble on the top right.

This diary is the property of Matilda Strangler

"Now we're talking. Mighty convenient, but it's about time these clues started to help me out. Clagton. Dells. Spells. No cow bells." Harry finished the Jaffa cake before cracking open the hazelnut and (milk) chocolate cookie, reading the now obligatory clue.

28 August 1682

An ode to the cow bell

Amidst the sound of orchestral string,
Of cymbal crash and tempestuous din,
There is one sound that stirs my heart,
That threatens the very seas to part,
Oh, noble cow bell —hear my cry,
Doth bring a melancholy tear to my eye,
So out of place yet without you it wouldst be,
A so very plain and unbalanced melody.

Harry turned the piece of paper over, before re-reading, turning the page upside-down and on its side. Finally, he shook his head. "Nope, what a complete waste of time." He added it to the small collection of pages he had already obtained, folding them in half and tucking them into the waistband of his speedos.

Crunching on the last half of the cookie, he closed the still-open chassis flap on BU-4T. "Right, so now we have a name. Can you cross-reference it with information from 1680-1682, census data, crow sightings, bulk iron purchases and narrow down a location of this mysterious lodge? I best get out there and see the lay of the land. It's evident that whatever happened back then could be happening again. At least if Barnaby is on the level, anyway."

The menacing robot blinked into life, uttering a single word before divulging the required information. "Affirmative."

That's what robots say, trust me, I spent three years as one in the very battle that BU-4T fought in. Hardest game in the world being a robot. Gone are yes and no, in are affirmative and negative. You don't want to get that muddled up or your new robot chums become suspicious and you'd be vaporised before you can recant your favourite binary solo.

What's mine? It's an old classic, called 01000100 01110101 01101110 01100011 01100001 01101110 00100000 01101001 01110011 00100000 01100111 01110010 01100101 01100001 01110100.

Ahh, great times, dear reader. Great times.

Chapter
Eight

Pyrethrum daisy

With the robot's information stored in his short-term memory, and a map stolen from the perpetually explorative Japanese couple, Mr and Mrs Kobe, Harry's plan consisted of heading to the location of the witch's lodge, or at least, where it had been, and try to find something to get this plot motoring on. He knew that little chance remained of the house still being there, three-and-a-bit centuries later (especially if the diary entries were true and the domicile had indeed been made out of baked goods).

Regardless, it was the only lead he had in this case, and with the victims piling up —not literally, they weren't being stacked in the hospital, that's a negligence case in waiting— it was a no-brainer to check out the veracity of the information he was being drip-fed by the mysterious Barnaby. With the modern map and the outlying directions provided in the information from the library, Harry was able to determine that this likely non-existent lodge was on the edge of a housing estate.

Climbing over a fence which acted as a border between Mercia Avenue and the fabled land, Harry found himself bollock-deep (that's actual nads, not books, in this case) in the Hampshire countryside. In the distance he could make out the edge of a forest, and before that lay a vast field which was covered in shoulder-height grass. It was now he regretted not having gone home and changed whilst he had the chance; as he stumbled blindly through the overgrown land his body became a homing beacon to stinging nettles, ticks and venomous sparrows which circled overhead.

It seemed pointless; this land had not seen a grass cull in years. Harry soon encountered a gang of feral children who had been abandoned into the wilderness as mere foetuses. Having bartered for his safe passage with the only currency he had —his blood— he forged deeper into the overgrowth. The sun was beginning to quit for the day and was slowly falling down, heading for tropical climes and people who still worshipped it as a god. With a pint-and-a-half less blood pumping around his veins, Harry began to slow, his head light and throbbing. "There's nothing out here." Then at the exact moment he was about to give up hope, it happened.

A bloodthirsty venomous sparrow broke ranks with its kin and dive-bombed the man utterly lost in the tall grass. The only warning the detective had was the signature cry of the bird as it neared its prey. From above, Harry heard, "incoming," in a high-pitched venomous sparrow screech. His leaden legs made the sudden descent to the ground considerably easier, sinking below the line of grass and out of sight. With its intended target gone, the sparrow pulled up and banked sharply to the right.

Harry pushed himself to all fours, scouting the sky above and seeing the damned bird lining up its next attack run. He knew that to stay where he was would be suicide. If the bird didn't get him, the children might, eager to exsanguinate him, having already yummed down the jug of blood he had given them.

Standing up, he began to jog, trying to pick a path out to the promise of sanctuary. The sparrow —now alienated from its gang for going alone— knew that it had to take the biped down. It would be the only way it could ingratiate himself back with its feathered pals. It saw its prey lope through the dense grass, heading for the forest, where the enclosed space from the tree trunks would render any chance of victory slim.

With his arms pumping like a steam train, albeit a very slow one, Harry kept going. Yet it felt like he was running on the spot, the horizon staying resolutely in the distance. He dared a look behind him and saw the sparrow line up for another try; this time there would be no escape. The detective put his head down and forced himself to go faster. As he felt his legs burn from the exertion, two of his senses picked up on odd things. The first was from his ears, which heard a WHOOSHING sound ahead of him, which then ripped past his head, near deafening him. The second was his nose twitching, the smell of wood varnish mixed with a faint essence of Madagascan Vanilla custard, being gently heated on the hob.

From his rear came a squawk. Harry glanced back to see that the sparrow had been taken out mid-flight by a sharpened herb breadstick, the quills made from venomous sparrow feathers; OH, THE IRONY. With his chance of pain-filled doom receding, Harry slowed down to a jog. A few more steps and he no longer felt the blades of grass whip against his legs, as it gave way to a large clearing.

Coming to a complete stop, he took in the vista, which was nothing spectacular; it certainly wouldn't be rendered in paint by Turner or Constable. His saviour was a woman, wearing clothing fabricated using only items which had been discarded by the denizens of the housing estate. She was wearing a lurid pink shell suit, an eye visor from nearby attraction The Shipton Bellinger Crypt, and plastic sandals which were near worn out. Taking time out to move something from one sack to another, she aimed a homemade bow at him; a mini baguette sharpened to a wicked point was nocked and loaded.

Behind her was a single storey shack on the verge of collapse. The house leaned to one side, buffeted by the wind and baked in place by the sun. Even from this distance, Harry could see that the walls were mouldy bread products. However, it had a shiny outer layer pasted over every exposed roll and bagel.

Then, as far as the eye could see, was a freshly harvested field. Harry knelt to examine one of the stalks, even with the improvised arrow aimed at his nether regions. Running a finger around the sundered stem, he gulped, noticing that the circumference was on a par with the flowers he had seen on each of the victims. Yet amongst these were other broken plant life. Some had the circumference of dinner plates, others were as large as hula hoops (the circular devices that go around your waist, not the crisps, for they would be rather tiny, really). "What is this place?" He asked the woman, her eyes shielded from the fading rays of the sun.

"Home."

"Who are you?" Harry stood up, dusting his hands together.

"Me."

"Not much of a conversationalist, are you?"

"No."

"Can you at least lower the shooter so I can ask you a few questions?"

"Okay," reluctantly, the woman unhitched the baguette and lowered the weapon.

With his heart rate slowly settling, Harry pointed at the rickety shack. "This place is real, then? I'm guessing you're a Strangler?"

With an imaginary arrow in the bow, the woman pulled the string back and let it go, shaking her head. "Firer."

Harry chuckled. "No, love. I meant are you related to Matilda Strangler?"

With a near toothless grin —lack of adequate dental provisions will do that to you, and there is little natural substitute for toothpaste— the woman nodded. "Yes."

"Ooh, feel like I'm making progress," Harry pulled the wad of paper from his trunks. "I've been reading about her, Matilda, can't believe her house was real. Was wondering how much of that diary was bullshit."

"Not bullshit."

"Wow, two words, we're cooking on gas now. You know about the diary, then? What went on with her and the villagers all those years ago?"

"Yes. I mean no."

"I *knew* I could squeeze some more words from you, I'll get a complete chapter from you in no time."

"What?"

"Nothing, just an in-joke with someone. So what happened to the diary, then?"

Sally shrugged.

"You do know that it's in your interests to help me, yeah? At the moment, all roads lead to Weirdsville. That's here, in case you were wondering. Between the diary pages, your family's history and the flowers, you're pretty much the only suspect."

"In what?"

"Playing the innocence game? Fair enough. I suppose I should thank you for saving me back there, thought I was a goner for sure."

"Bread," the woman tapped the baguette arrow, cured no doubt from a broken piece of witch's lodge wall.

"An unusual choice in warfare. Sun Tzu didn't reference it in his fancy manual. Okay, an obvious question I suppose, how has your bread-house not fallen apart?"

"Varnish."

Harry sniffed the air again. "Ah, of course, kinda obvious really when you think about it."

"Yes."

"Don't get clever with me, you hand-me-down-wearing slag."

The woman aimed the bow at Harry again. "Be nice."

"Fair enough," Harry gestured to the freshly harvested field. "Is this all yours?"

She tapped her chest with her thumb, "Sally."

"Sally…is this your land? Did you grow things here? Look, there are people being afflicted by something weird in Charlton—"

"Charlton?" The woman rolled the letters around her mouth like they were animal bones in a wooden bowl of divination.

(That's a Grade-A witch joke, by the way.)

"Sorry, Clagton. They're being hurt by flowers; do you know anything about it?"

Sally shook her head. "Not me."

"Really? Look around you, where are all the crops that grew here? The flowers, where are they? The diary mentioned them too. I think you know more than you're letting on. Why won't you just tell me what you know?"

"Don't know anything." Releasing the baguette once more, Sally grabbed hold of the sacks and dragged them back to her varnished bread hovel. As she wrenched open the door, she looked Harry straight in the eyes, "*not* me."

"Hold on there, Missy." Harry jogged over to the woman. Plunging a hand into the fatter of the two sacks, his hand came out clutching wads of rolled up banknotes. "Hey, where did you get this moolah from? There must be thousands here."

"Found it," Sally slapped the detective's hands and chucked the cash back into its dank home.

"You found this?"

"Yes."

"Where?"

Sally pointed to a patch of flattened grass. "There."

Having rescued the money and distracted the detective, Sally ducked through the doorway, slammed the door shut and braced it with a giant French stick. Harry slapped his cheek as a fly tried to have sex with his beard follicles. "Found them? A likely story, my arse." On clue, his rectum began to vibrate, and he could feel stirrings within. On the cusp of climax, he remembered the source. Delving around —but allowing enough time to finish off what it had started— Harry retrieved his pager. He read the message out. "Harry. STOP. Get back to hospital. STOP. Specialist here. STOP. Has information. STOP." Slipping it back into his special bum-pocket he took one last look at the scene before picking his way back through the grass and to civilisation beyond. Determined that when he saw Dr. Singh, he would explain that a pager and a telegram are two very different things. Both archaic and outdated methods for sure, but he really ought to know the difference between the two.

STOP.

Chapter Nine

Brunnera macrophylla

By the time the ambulance bay doors opened for Harry, he was clutching another half-dozen wrapped biscuits. He was getting pissed off with the whole plot delivery device now, and was looking forward to getting actual information from a specialist in their field rather than a jumped-up toff who hand-delivered biscuits from peculiar places.

(Who remembers those halcyon days?)

Before he had a chance to go through his pager/telegram spiel with Dr. Singh, the sheer multitude of people in the waiting room hit him. Well, their body odour did, along with their grating voices and panic levels as they shared scurrilous rumour and unsupported theories. Harry's favourite was from a rotund gentleman with no earlobes, who told his young daughter that her mummy "had frequented with typewriter ribbons one time too many," and this was the direct reason why a flower was covering her mouth and nose. The little girl knew this to be bollocks but realised that arguing the point with her flat-earth believing father was useless.

Harry slapped his palm against the doors to the Intensive Recovery Wing, which he could see had been extended and renovated since his last visit.

Where before there were only two bays, a building contractor had fitted another twelve, each with their full complement of medical equipment and vengeful spirit. Dr. Singh waved his key card at the panel, and the doors opened. A tide of worried family members rolled up to the cavernous entry point, which led Singh to keeping them at arm's length with his trusty bullwhip and chair usually reserved for herding the pregnant or infirm.

"Looks like you've been busy," Harry stated the obvious, seeing that the doctor was already two days into his standard eight-day shift and all the life support machines were doing a merry jig of going BING. They were slightly out of sync, which made for a mesmerising peal of BINGs rippling around the bays.

"All of them are the same, not a damn difference between any of them. I almost…I almost…"

"What?" Harry peeked through the curtains at Natasha, patient zero-plus-one. She remained serene, asleep, still covered in all manner of sensors and stickers from fruit.

Singh lowered his voice, keen to avoid being picked up by the microphones which report everything back to the Cupboard People —the ones who really run the government. "I almost want one of them to die," he tittered, covering his mouth with his hands like a mouse trying to shove in all his stolen cheese before the Cheese Police arrived. You know, after the largest cheese heist in Mouseville had just gone down.

"Why? Are they pissing you off? Are their stupid fucking faces with that stupid fucking flower on, getting on your testes?"

"No. It's not that."

"Then what?"

"People round here would give me a cool nickname, you know? Like Killer Doc, or Vengeful Venkatesh. Be better than what they call me now."

"Which is? Bear in mind that I'm only speaking to you now out of sheer and total fucking boredom. You know. Because you bore me. To near death."

"They call me the Milk Sniffer."

"Could be worse."

Singh looked up, shocked. "Really?"

"Course, they could call you Fucking Boring Arsehole Rimjobber Extraordinaire. From Kettering."

The doctor snapped his fingers. "You're right. Milk Sniffer isn't too bad after all. Although…"

"What? This is going to be some gross revelation, isn't it?"

"It's breast milk."

"And there we go. Though breast milk isn't terrible, I know some people who drink nut milk, you know, from almonds, not testicles. What utter lunatics."

"It's dog's breast milk."

Harry patted him on the shoulder, although he was initially apprehensive about being tactile with a man who wasn't a blood relation and who inhaled canine lactations. "That's my twat."

"What's it doing there? Won't it get dusty?"

Harry pinched the doctor's shoulder. "Enough. You paged me, remember? Said that the specialist was here with some actual fucking information? Please tell me they're still here and you haven't either bored them to death or euthanised them in order to grope up another rung on the medical ladder."

The curtain opposite swished open. A stern-looking woman wearing a lab coat and a gas mask swept from the bay. In one hand she held a pair of pliers and in the other, a double-blank domino tile. She lifted the gas mask, exposing a mouth that was shorn of lips. "You must be Detective Surge."

Harry clicked his heels together, which was silly, as he had no shoes on and his bony feet spurs cracked together like two rocks. "And you must be mother. Good job, there are some sheets that need ironing."

The woman slapped him across the cheek, leaving the domino tile embedded in his ear canal. "I am Doctor Petula Finklesmitt, botanist to the stars, shrubbery pruner of the rich and famous, and the creator of the wheeled watering can."

Fiddling with the tile —but deciding that he'd best leave it in on the off-chance the woman had lodged it in his weak spot— Harry carefully removed his sunglasses. One of the lenses hung out of the frame after the impact. "And owner of a mean right hook. Mind if I call you slugger?"

"Only if you want to be unable to walk. On account of you having lost both your legs to my diamond-toothed hedge trimmer."

"Fair point. Well made. So, what news do you bring? Please tell me you have something, I need some cold hard facts ..." Harry tipped the biscuits onto a metal tray, "... which aren't the diary excerpts of a seventeenth century witch. Probably."

Petula shoved the pliers into her coat pocket and ran her tongue over her teeth —which were permanently exposed to the air. "It's a type of orchid, that much is evident, from the *Furem* branch, a rare strain that is only found in a few remaining idylls."

"What the fuck is a Furem, when it's at home? Not like a sex spray, is it?"

"That's *pheromone*, you imbecile, no. Furem means thief in Latin."

"Ahhh, course, Latin. The dead language that just refuses to take the fucking hint."

"As I was saying…it was long believed that the Furem strain had died out completely, this is the first time I've seen one in the flesh, so to speak, and even then I will need to conduct more tests to find out exactly what we're dealing with."

"Why is that exactly? Surely a flower is a flower?"

"For many, maybe, but this belongs to a particular type of flora which —although pollinated like any other— has some curious habits."

"Like latching onto people's faces?"

"That's the thing, there has never been a recorded instance of this, though this plant has been found suckling on wildlife and sometimes their own kind. If I was to propose an outrageous supposition, I'd say that this is a hybrid; someone or something has spliced its genetic make-up with something else, to what end I don't know for sure just yet."

Harry pinched the bridge of his nose, yearning for the days when he would receive his clues in biscuit form. "Fucking hell, Doc, I thought you said this woman knew what was going on? All I'm hearing is blah blah cunty bullshit blah."

Petula ran a finger over her teeth, sticking what remained of her inside gums to her ivory pegs. "I can only tell you what I know, and what I know is that these plants should not be stuck to a human's face. No good is going to come of it. If I had to speculate even further, I'd say that although the stem is currently enabling the victim to breathe, that could change at any given moment. If it closes, and the stigmas and petal retract any more, then asphyxiation will occur."

"You saying that these are killer flowers? Like Triffids?" Dr. Singh butted in.

"Possibly. We have to look at the facts. Every person who gets near the flower reports different aromas, it's always the thing that person longs for the most in a scent."

"What do you smell, then?" Harry asked, genuinely interested for once.

"From the trace amounts emanating from the gaps, I detected notes of thimble glaze and sun-dried foreskins."

"Kinky."

"Quite. The flower appears to be designed with the explicit purpose of attracting people to smell them, to make them irresistible to their target, yet at the time appearing to be something different to everyone else. Then, with the target breathing in, the stigma latches onto the inner nostril with small barbs which pierce the thin flesh and administer a strong anaesthetic, rendering the person unconscious.

"They really are extraordinary. I've tried peeling open the petals, and although I have managed to gain access, it is only temporary. I've had to study the workings for one or two second intervals over the space of the last forty minutes. Then they snap shut, pulling the face closer to ensure a better seal."

"But why? What are they doing this for? There has to be an end game. Where the hell have they come from?" Dr. Singh rattled off his questions.

Harry smirked. "I think I know *where*. There's a field out by the back of Mercia Avenue. In a clearing, there are tens, hundreds of cut stems."

Petula took in a breath, pulling her gums tighter over her teeth. "How did you find them?"

"Our mystery biscuit benefactor. It's almost like he's trying to purposely lead me there, again, no idea as to his motives. Could be a do-gooder, but there's no way anyone can know as much as he does and not be involved in some way. I need to find…or *fabricate* some evidence so I can introduce him to my favourite camera-free cell back at the station and a nice gravel enema I have prepared for just such an eventuality."

"Regardless, we have to look at the facts. At the moment, the cases are steadily increasing, if the numbers you're talking about are true, then it's clear that whoever is behind this is looking to infect as many people as possible."

Harry smacked a fist into his palm. "Maybe even the whole village?"

"It's possible, though it would be highly improbable that a high percentage of the population would be able to be affected by this. If we put out a warning, there's no way this would spread too far, then we just deal with these people and hope for the best."

"Only one small problem…" Petula pulled out a folded piece of paper from her pocket.

Unfolding it, Harry's face dropped. "My god, this is today?"

"What is it?" Singh asked.

Harry passed the crumpled flyer across to the doctor, who joined the man in face-dropping shock. "No, it can't be."

"Today is the annual summer fete, down at the village hall. Prizes on offer for the biggest vegetables …" He paused for dramatic effect, "…and finest flowers."

"You don't think?"

"If someone went to the trouble of putting these orchids in the local shop, then it's only natural that whoever is behind this would see this as the perfect means of widespread delivery. This could infect most of the villagers in one devilish move. I've got to get down there. You, find out more about these flowers, are they going to kill, or will they eventually just drop off?" Harry shooed Petula into the nearest bay.

"What shall I do, Detective?" Singh asked.

Harry bit off the end of a cigar and spat it out. "Pray."

"Oh. I'm not a religious man."

"Then order me a taxi. Fucking hell, it's like I have to do everything myself."

"You want me to order a taxi? Really? I'm a trained medical professional."

The detective held out his badge. "Sod it, it's time I abused my lofty position of authority. Out of the way, peasant. I'm going to go outside, and the first vehicle I see? I'm going to commandeer the fuck out of it." Storming out through the main entrance —which conveniently also doubled up as an exit - just don't tell the door's boss as it's claiming overtime for both on the sly he did indeed point at the first vehicle he saw, shouting, "You there, stop in the name of the law. I need to use your transportation as this is a case of life and death. If you deny me, it'll be your death. So pony up the keys, you vehicle-driving prick."

Chapter
Ten

Rosa 'Eden'

The blimp for Roxy's Tyres was perhaps not the best mode of transportation. Granted, it wasn't a huge distance to traverse, but I'll let you in on something…come closer. CLOSER. So close that the words near blur into one and you have difficulty making them out. Now move back slightly. Ready? Okay, here we go.

Blimps aren't that fast.

Blew your mind a little there, didn't I? It's true, though, and if you don't believe me, what are you going to do? Not as if you can hire one and take it round the block, eh? You can go back to reading at optimal distance now, whatever works best for you.

Harry pulled open the door and peered down past the ledge of the cockpit. Below him was the tell-tale sign of the village hall. Some of the bored youth had painted VILLAGE HALL on the roof in bright orange paint a few years back to the consternation of many, but those people were lazy sods, and cleaning it up was still on their to-do list along with repairing the downstairs toilet which had been rendered inoperable after an obstinate blockage.

Nothing to do with me.

For once.

Anyway…

Having fashioned a length of rope from the internal cabling of non-important systems —and let's face it, it's a zeppelin, hardly a technological marvel now, is it?— Harry tied one end to the driver's seat and the other around his waist. He hoped the length was correct, else he'd be either left dangling like a right dickhead or meeting the floor at speed sufficient enough to turn him from alive to dead.

Paying minimal credence to the wind conditions, Harry dived out of the blimp and clasped his hands together, aiming for the road that ran outside the village hall. The ground was growing ever bigger, ever faster and it was just when he achieved terminal velocity that he wished he had quit giving it the big 'un to Dr. Singh and had just agreed to getting a taxi. His fears were allayed as the cable pulled taut at a near perfect length. After a brief dangle as he tried to untie the knot around his waist, he landed on the floor with something akin to balletic grace.

"This is going to be a piece of piss," he muttered to his own reflection in his mirrored sunglasses, before putting them back on and cracking his fingers. Through a bushy hedgerow, which permitted a narrow passage through to the path leading to the village hall entrance beyond, Harry could see that the doors were open, and that there was human life.

By life, I mean the burly frame of Todd, the village bouncer. Any event, big or small, you'll find Todd doing the security. He refused me entrance to my cousin's kid's christening once; he's a proper officious bastard. As will be demonstrated thus.

"Alright, Todd." Harry gave a brief salute and made to enter the building.

Todd's arms were folded across his body in no time at all, and he side-stepped across from his temporary standing position, allowing people to leave, to full on *thou shall not pass*.

"You got a ticket, Harry?"

"Sure thing, let me just get it for you." Harry patted himself down before giving him the finger. "There you go. As you can see, it admits one, now get the fuck out of my way."

Todd shook his head, puffing his pork pie chest up even further, his arms swallowed up by the flesh expansion. "That's not a ticket. That's your middle finger."

"Well done Fatty Boom-Boom, now do one, I'm on important police business."

His hand —retrieved from his bulk— was shoved into Harry's naked chest. "No ticket. No entry. Besides, I thought you got suspended by the cops on account of you defecating on the Chief Constable's kitten?"

"I'll tell you what I told those jumped up pussies at the tribunal. That fucking cat got what it deserved. Digging up my garden, crapping in my spare shoes. You hear me? My spare fucking shoes. Ruined by that little sod."

"You didn't need to chase it down and truss it up with masking tape before dropping your guts all over it."

Harry pulled his shades off. "I don't need to explain myself to you. I shat on a cat, that's all. This is a fucking emergency! I've received information that the people inside are in peril. Not mild peril. Extreme fucking terrorist level shit peril."

Todd eyed him up. "I didn't hear any sirens. If it's so desperate, how did you get here?"

Harry pointed to the cloud-pocked sky, the blimp careening off into the distance at four knots, in danger of bumping into absolutely nothing. "That."

"Ah, a dirigible."

"I do ridge a bull? What does that even mean?"

"No. Dirigible."

"Speaking slower doesn't make the Rubik's cube easier to solve, you fat fuck."

"Di-"

"Do."

"-rig-"

"Ridge."

"-i-"

"A."

"-ble."

"Bull."

"Dirigible."

"Do ridge a bull. What are you on about? Is this from your latest book? Are you using author words on me?"

"No, *dirigible*, it's another word for a blimp."

"Then why didn't you just say blimp?" Harry clawed at his own face, trying to look past the man into the village hall interior, seeing nothing but children's shitty pictures covering the stained-glass windows. One of them was signed Beht Milse. "Figures his progeny would be as stupid."

"If I said blimp, you might've taken the mickey out of my weight again."

"LET ME IN, YOU OBESE MOTHERFUCKER."

"Not without a ticket. Rules are rules, you'd know this if you didn't spend half your life trying to break them."

Harry sighed. He knew there was no way past this stickler for detail, having heard what happened to me at my cousin's kid's christening. "How much?"

"A quid."

Rooting around inside of his purse —which was also up his arse— Harry accidentally tugged on his colon. Finally retrieving the entry fee, he licked it, slapped it into Todd's outstretched hand, and barged past. "Notice anything odd inside?"

Expertly swapping money for a ticket stub, Todd moved out of the way. "Not really, though from the smell, I think my mum's in there baking my favourite meal, liver on toast."

"Oh god no…" Harry kicked open the door, feeling naked without his trusty trebuchet, having left it in the back of that ambulance a few chapters back. What was I thinking? He could've used that right about now, but for my incompetence.

The door flew open, a thick waft of gently cooked (on the hob) Madagascan Vanilla custard smothering him with its loveliness. In the background, the strains of Mozart's Requiem Mass in D minor echoed the futility of his hope. If you want to be fully immersed in the remainder of this scene, why not play it in accompaniment?

Strewn all over the floor were the local parishioners, every last one of them with an orchid hugging the lower half of their face. "I'm too late …"

The music faded for the briefest of moments, to allow a TOOT-TOOT from the road beyond. A sound that came not from a man-made object, but from a human throat.

"Not him!" Harry pushed past Todd, who realised that this was going to look very bad on his CV, and through the gap in the hedgerow which felt like it was going to envelop him in its twigs and barbs. Sure enough, parked on the curb was Barnaby, riding the motorcycle side of a motorbike and sidecar combination.

"I've got a wee delivery for you, detective, I do hope you have a sweet tooth." Barnaby flashed a smile and pulled the canvas roof off the sidecar. Harry stumbled towards it; his mouth wide open. Stacked inside the sidecar was a selection of biscuits, all individually wrapped, all no doubt containing yet more words from Matilda Strangler. Witch. Denizen of Clagton. Part-time wishing well. Rubbish at noticing that her cat was a tarred chicken with wooden prosthetics.

Barnaby unhitched the motorbike from the sidecar and tilted his top hat before tearing off down the road. Harry was trying to work out which baked delight to start with when he heard a thud behind him. Ducking through the groping hedge, he saw Todd lying unconscious on the floor, face down. To get him into the recovery position, Harry put the bouncer's arms by his side and rolled him over. He gasped; Todd too had succumbed to the dreaded Furem orchid.

"But how can that be?" Harry noted that the man had appeared to be trying to get away before he had been attacked. "How was that even possible, unless…" The detective stepped over Todd, and with his bruised big toe hooked around the door, pulled it back gently. As he did, he saw a flower head crane its neck round the bottom of the doorframe. That was odd, admittedly, but then the bloody thing looked up at him, its petals quivering before the twin stigmas exploded in a mass of tiny tentacles.

"Shit."

Harry retracted his foot, hoping that the door would either push the flower back in or crush it beneath its wooden trim. Besides, the flower hadn't *really* moved. Had it? "Of course not. That would be silly." Still, as the door closed, a green leaf flicked out and held it open.

"Shit."

Before he knew it, the orchid had flicked open the door, crouched down and leapt for the detective's face. Acting purely on instinct (and the ninja training he obtained during his sabbatical in Hyogo province), Harry swatted the flying flower from the air with the back of his hand. It landed neatly on its stem on Todd's back —as if it had grown from the bouncer's spine. Each leaf flickered outwards, as if brushing itself down, before beckoning Harry forward.

Harry snapped forward and dislocated Todd's left arm from its socket before ripping it clean off, ducking backwards as the orchid tried to latch onto his face. Armed with…erm…an *arm*, Harry felt empowered. As the flower hopped off the stricken bouncer —now bleeding out onto the gravel path— it jumped from side to side, trying to find a gap in the detective's defence.

Determined not to let the orchid settle, Harry lashed out with the severed appendage, catching the flower on its side petals despite it trying to duck out of the way. This only served to enrage the thing, which sprung off the ground and onto Harry's own arm. The detective stepped backwards instinctively, catching his heel on a loose border stone and falling to the ground, his weapon buried within the hedge.

Trying to shake the stars from his eyes, Harry could feel the flower crawl up his arm, hiking across his bicep as if it were an inconvenient mound of flesh, bone and sinew. Which it is. Silly analogy really, but I like it. Harry's head tipped to regard his doom, as the flower head opened up, each stigma unfurling slowly again for effect, the tiny barbs catching the last rays of sunlight. As he prepared for contact, there was only one thing running through his brain. *Mmm, that custard smells lovely.*

From the edge of his peripheral vision came a brown blur, which connected with the orchid mere inches from closing around Harry's mouth and nose. The blur resolved itself into a shoe, which led to an ankle, and then a leg. A whole ruddy leg, with trousers wrapped around it. This led to…

Oh, for fuck's sake, it was a person, okay? I know you *know* where the leg leads to, but you want to know who's leg it was, especially given Harry's breathless gasp as the foot came down on the stricken flower head as it tried to right itself and was crushed utterly underfoot.

Damn close, huh?

You want to know who saved him from certain unconsciousness? Just you wait and see, the answer will shock you.

Well probably not, as there's only a finite number of characters that have been introduced so far. Have a quick think about who you reckon it is and see if you're right shortly.

Chapter
Eleven

Nigella damascena

A whole chapter reserved for you to contemplate who saved Detective Harry Surge from the mysterious Os Furem orchid. Here's an artist's impression of me at a party, which acts as a kind of mental palette cleanser.

Chapter
Twelve

Lathyrus odoratus

A hand reached down for Harry, who took it gladly. Once on his feet, the detective looked from pulped flower to Todd, who already had an emergency tourniquet applied to his upper arm. "You can thank me, you know?" The enigmatic benefactor said, winking.

It was a bit awkward, to be honest; Harry didn't know if it was intentional or a nervous tic. Finally regaining the power of speech, he asked. "Thanks, you're the last person I expected. How did you know I was here?" Before they had a chance to answer, an orchid which had been loitering in the upper eaves of the village hall porchway took its chance and pounced, landing on Harry's saviour.

"Smells like crayons sitting on a wobbly paving slab," were their solitary words before they collapsed into the hedgerow and sunk to the ground.

Harry picked himself up and shook himself down. As he went to check on the latest victim, he heard a familiar sound from the road, TOOT-TOOT. Turning to look through the gap, he saw Barnaby deposit two more biscuits into the sidecar collection before he clipped his cane against his hat brim and disappeared.

"This is getting beyond a joke now." Harry ducked back into the street and jogged the short distance to a red telephone box. Amazed it was still working, he dialled 999. "This is Detective Surge, listen to me carefully. I'm at Charlton Village hall and there's been a mass attack. You have got to warn everyone that these fucking flowers can move by themselves. I know,

I barely believed it myself, but it's true. There are around a hundred or so affected, we need to get them to hospital, like now. So get anything you can, I commandeered a ridge a bull so get some coaches, fuck, I don't care how you do it, just get down here and get these poor sons of bitches outta there. You get all that?"

There was a brief pause at the other end of the line, before a voice said, "Which emergency service do you require?"

Harry squeezed the receiver, the plastic squeaking in resistance. "I'm not repeating myself, sweetheart, play it back if you have to, but—"

"Which emergency service do you require? Police. Fire, or…" the voice became muffled, no doubt a hand placed over the receiver. "…yeah, I know. Didn't even think she liked him, but what can you do? Amazed she didn't just marinate him there and then." Finally, the voice cleared and added, "…ambulance?"

"Look, I-"

"Coastguard?"

"-just get down-"

"Jar opener?"

"-fuck sake, why-"

"Spider remover?"

On the verge of losing his temper, Harry hit the receiver against the palm of his hand. He had to do something, and now. There had to be a way to get this damn person to leap into action, so he clicked his fingers. "There are vouchers for free sports massages down here, just waiting to be picked up."

There was a sharp intake of breath from the operator, and some hushed words. "Understood, Detective, a specialist retrieval team will be with you shortly."

Harry chuckled. "I thought they might."

He was about to put the phone down when the voice asked. "Are there any vouchers for Indian head massages too? My migraines have been sheer hell this past—"

Chapter
Thirteen

Lavandula

"Just stack them on top of each other," Dr. Singh called out over the din. The builders had failed to return and add an annexe to the extension they had built earlier, so he had to think on his feet. With so many patients being delivered at once via a donkey-train which stretched all the way down the hill to the village hall, he knew space would be at a premium.

"No, fold the feet out on the stretchers first, then lift with your knees and rest them on the stretcher below. Be quick." Singh ushered Harry forward. "Got there too late, then?"

"No, of course not, Doc. These are all extras in the film of your life, I've paid them to look as though they're unconscious, when really they're just pretending."

"Really? They look genuinely subdued to me."

Harry looked to the light fitting above him in the vain hope of it imparting some inner resolve. It failed, so he had to fall back to a further dose of sarcasm and rudeness. "Of *course* they're genuine, you dog-milk-sniffing dickhead. How the fuck am I going to get this lot to piss around when the stakes are so high?"

Singh wiped away a tear. "Your words hurt, detective."

"Boo-fucking-hoo, look, this shit is not only real but getting worse, the bloody things are mobile. If it wasn't for—"

The doors to the intensive care unit opened with a hiss. Petula threw a bone saw at the men, missing both but lancing a nasty boil which had come up on young William Thacker's knee. "Thank you, Miss," the child shouted before mopping up the dribbling pus with his school jumper and irritating people in the way that only a freshly-lanced child can.

"Gentlemen, something is happening, you best come in and see."

The trio stood over Natasha, who was still laying perfectly still, yet the machine which measured her heart rate and indignation levels was tracing lines on the screen which defied convention. Singh tapped a finger against his lips. "My, this defies all convention."

See. I tried telling you.

Petula tugged the hem of Harry's trunks, threatening to disrobe him. "Detective, I've made a breakthrough in my investigation. As I feared, these flowers are indeed hybrids."

"What does that even mean? They use petrol *and* electric?"

The woman shook her head. "No. That's cars. Natasha is a person; she has none of the components which would classify her as an automobile."

"Righto. So what exactly are you babbling on about?"

Singh moved to Natasha's side. Her skin was clammy, a spike on the new-phobia monitor caused the machine to BEEP incessantly. Ignoring her perspiration, he clamped his fingers on her wrist, trying to find a pulse. It was there alright, but it too was banging about like an over-caffeinated drum machine from a Grebo band in the early nineties. Pressing his digits firmer into her wrist, his eyes widened as he felt something move within. "Erm…guys?"

Petula had pulled out a whiteboard and was explaining the process of how different species could exchange parts of their genetic make-up and in turn create completely new strains of themselves, with new characteristics. "… but in this case, someone has tampered with the genetic code of the orchid. Tell me, Detective, how *is* your Latin?"

"Non est bonum," Harry replied.

"Do you know what Furem translates to?"

Singh raised his voice. "Guys, something is happening here," he said, his fingers sliding up and down Natasha's arm as it pulsed and writhed.

Harry held up a hand to the doctor. "No, I don't know what it translates to. Why don't you illuminate me?"

Turning back to the whiteboard, Petula said. "It means thief." She wrote two letters on the board, which formed one word. They're cool like that.

"Os? What the fuck is that? Is it like Windows 95?"

Petula laughed and tipped her head back, flicking the back of her hair from side to side as if she were trying to gently evict a family of hair worms. "No…detective. It means—"

"FOR PETE'S SAKE YOU TWO, IT'S HER BONE," Singh shouted, utterly frustrated with the pair of them.

"Correct," Petula replied, ceasing her hair shaking and underlining *Os Furem* on the whiteboard three times.

"It's what? Pete? Os is Latin for Pete? That's odd. I thought it was Petrum."

"It is."

"What is?"

Petula shoved the marker pen in her pocket. "Petrum is Latin for Peter."

Harry sighed. "I know. What does Os mean?"

Singh smacked a brain scooper against the metal bar which stops people from rolling out of bed and into the bottomless pit of dread. "You two, it's her damn bone."

"Correct," Petula added again, hands in pockets, partaking in the rare female pastime of enjoying wearing an item of clothing with pockets.

"FOR FUCK'S SAKE," Harry shouted. "You two are doing my head in. Let's take this in turns. Doctor, what in the name of hairy ballbags are you going on about? Quid pro quo, Petrum is Latin for Peter, okay?" Singh held up Natasha's arm, his fingers pinched into her skin, which was bulging out wider than it should. "Fucking hell, what's up with her arm?" Harry asked.

"It's what I've been trying to tell you. Her arm bone, the radius, which runs on the outside of the forearm…it's …it's gone!"

"Where did you see it last?" Harry looked under and over the stretcher, seeing if the Doctor had mislaid it, like an errant marker pen.

"Nowhere. I haven't lost it, it's just gone."

"How?"

"I don't know. I was taking her pulse when it just disappeared, as if it was being pulled—"

"There it is!" Harry shouted, pointing at Natasha's upper arm, which bulged out at the bicep. Beneath her skin, the radius was sliding between epidermis and muscle, up towards the shoulder. "How are you doing that, Doc? You got some twine or something in there?"

Singh shook his head. "It's not me, you buffoon."

"You using a magnet?"

"It's not made of metal."

"Where's it going, then?" Harry winced as the bone worked its way up and over the shoulder, nearly bursting through the skin at one point.

Petula coughed. "May I interject?"

"Of course, it's your turn anyway, though you're going to have to go some to top the Doc's fucking disgusting arm bone trick."

"Os Furem means Bone Thief."

Harry pulled his shades off, rubbed his eyes with the back of his hands, and shouted, "WHAT?"

He'd obviously not read the title of the book. Sorry, *bollock*.

Petula crossed her arms. "The flowers, these orchids. In their original state they would latch on to trees and other plants, pulling strips of the flora into their very being, hence their bulbous stem. These, though…they've grown, evolved. They no longer crave sap or bark; they yearn for something quite, quite different."

"Human bones, by any chance?" Harry asked.

"Well yes, was hoping I'd get a bit more time to build up to the big reveal, but fine, go and steal my thunder, why don't you?" Petula put the marker pen in her pocket, intent on stealing it. At this juncture, the three of them stood in hushed silence while the radius bone pushed Natasha's neck to one side as it rounded the corner from torso to throat. Her back arched, flower still fastened to her face. Her head reddening, her cheeks and neck rippled as the bone was sucked onwards.

The trio peered into the hollow stem.

There was an audible pop, and at the far end of the stem, like a straw sucking up vanilla milkshake, a white blockage appeared. It grew and grew, easing the pressure on Natasha's head and causing the flower stem to puff out. As Natasha sagged back onto her pillow and her vital signs began to level out, Harry dabbed his finger against the end of the white object protruding from the bottom of the orchid. "Bony."

"I've never seen this before," Singh murmured.

"No-one has, at least it's never been recorded," Petula added.

Harry clicked his fingers. "Maybe not in your fancy books, but I reckon I know someone who has." He turned around to the pile of biscuits that he had dumped inside a vitally important baby incubator, the only one of its kind in the county.

Chapter
Fourteen

Origanum majorana

"I'm really rather full," Petula complained.

"Less bleating, more eating," Harry commanded. His guts rumbled as stomach acid struggled to break down yet more baked delights. Finishing off a Malted Milk, he flung the paper from the innards onto a surgical tray, which had been requisitioned as a clue deposit station.

"I think I'm going to be sick, there's too many. I really should be getting back to my patients." Singh eyed up a Fig Roll —loosely classified as a biscuit because I'm running out of choices— before reclining on the chair.

"What good will it do? Huh? Keen to witness it again? Once you've seen one arm bone being sucked up through the human physiology, you've seen 'em all. No, we stay here. Keep eating. The proof we need is in these biscuits that Barnaby keeps dropping off, it just has to be." Harry let out a burp before tucking into a sweet lemon cream.

On cue, Barnaby ducked his head around the corner. "Another batch of wonderful clue cookies for you." He turned his hat upside down, and another delivery fell onto Natasha's bed. Tapping the top of the hat, a final straggler plopped out before the man bid them adieu.

Petula forced herself to stand and stumbled across to the bed. "I don't see why we have to eat them all, why can't we just break them open and get the diary pages out?"

Harry slapped her across the face. "Heretic. No one besmirches the noble biscuit." He looked from the stack of paper to the mountain of wrapped biscuits that threatened to engulf patient zero entirely. "Mind you, we could be here for some time —and that's one thing we don't have. Stand down, people, we should have enough to move the plot forward."

Both Petula and Dr. Singh collapsed to the ground, their jaws tired from chewing, their blood sugar levels elevated. Taking his opportunity to leave, Singh headed out to the corridor to check on the latest batch of victims that had been dropped off.

"Come on, you bastard, where's my incriminating evidence when I need it?" Harry flicked through the pages, stopping at certain sentences and paragraphs as he went through.

I've found this particular flower to be most receptive to manipulation. Early tests led to it stripping a section of the east wall away. It not only attached itself to the wall with little fuss, but after some time it also extracted the dry bread from its interior. How can I use this against those infernal villagers?

Using my grandmother's recipe, I managed to prepare a hearty stew using only mandrake root, frog spit, moonlight and some interpretative dance. This should tide me over until the season of rebirth.

The change in weather threatens to destroy my hovel. I need more granary slices to shore up a roof collapse, using jam as mortar was ill-advised, as a family of preserve ants made short work of my attempts to repair the damage.

"You found anything yet?" Petula asked. She had sliced open her stomach and was bailing out semi-digested…erm…*digestives* from her guts using a china cup.

"Shh. Working."

I have it at last. I shall mix my intended revenge over the villagers with the malaise affecting my home. A few modifications to the orchid, and I think I can extract something from them which will serve me well.

Today I mourn. In my fevered efforts to perfect the latest strain of the flower, my trusty cat, Damian, was afflicted. With my knowledge of horticultural splicing still being in its infancy, instead of harvesting one particular element, every bone within his feline body was sucked out through the attachment point and into the flower.

Two graves did I dig. One for his outer coating and the other for the flower, which did not relinquish its bounty. Whilst I am devastated beyond words, this shall serve as adequate fuel to fan the flames of my hatred. They will not be delivered unto death. Neigh. For that would be too quick a blessing. No, I have something far more suiting of them.

Using the last of my child-catching baskets and an assortment of Lady Fingers, I was able to trap three children who had been sulking around my property. They will be the perfect subjects for my first tests on the human physiology.

Alas, the first test did not go as I wished. The child, a girl of around seven years in age, succumbed to the flower. I was unsure as to the point of connection and discovered to her cost that it should not be the ear. Eager to please me, the orchid sucked out her key organs alphabetically, squeezing one out on the hour every hour, until her plaintive screams allowed the neighbourhood wolves to sleep a deep slumber. I shall try once more.

Some success at last. I managed to mix the flower with an octopus that I found in a shallow rockpool. The stigmas were transformed into groping arms which nearly ensnared me. However, whilst this delivery method was perfect for latching onto the subject, who swore it smelled of their mother's favourite tunic, the flower once more emptied the child completely, turning it into little more than a hollow husk before daybreak. I feel so close. On the plus side, I now have a new lampshade. It is rather fetching, if a little too large.

Finally, my retribution is at hand. Child number three is recovering in the leech swamp out back. The flower *separated from them as hoped shortly after extraction, although I had to chase after it and slice open the stem to retrieve its bounty. One shiny arm bone. The flower unsurprisingly expired, its motor functions an unexpected, yet potentially welcome side effect, especially when it comes to harvesting my future yield.*

Harry stood up slowly, crumbs, plastic wrappings and paper tumbling from his body onto the floor. "Oh, fuck," Was all he could mutter before he fled out of the medical wing, the last piece of paper twirling through the air. Careful to not spill all her slippery guts onto the floor, Petula picked up the sheaf with blood-slicked fingers.

With my flowers casting their affections upon the villagers, I shall collect a solitary bone from every man, woman and child, and thanks to my grace, all shall live to look upon my creation with fear and shame, for they were the ones who turned me from peace to hatred. So shall it be that I will use their bones to build me a new home. One that will stand the test of time. One that my descendants shall use and call their own.

"Oh buggeration."

Chapter
Fifteen

Myosotis

Harry didn't have the *why*, but he had the who and the what figured out. As he bounced through the field, and the evening sky started to bleed every last ounce of colour into the horizon, he knew he was on the right track. "The witch with the flowers, in the field," he mumbled.

Fury and indignation were fuelling his journey on a purloined Space Hopper, from the hospital back to the clearing; he had gone past the stage of being pissed off having to trek back and forth between the same locales. Titbits of information baked inside a veritable selection box of biscuits weren't an issue either; he loved biscuits. If the delivery method had been bananas, for example, he might very well have an axe to grind with the narrative, but it wasn't, so he didn't.

No, the one thing that was bugging the hell out of him was the *why*. Sally was a little vocally challenged, and he had no doubt that living in a varnished bread house was bound to cause a litany of medical conditions and ailments. But why the fuck had she decided to try to re-enact the past? Had Charlton's villagers been mistreating her? He hadn't heard anything, but then he'd been suspended for a month now, so the only reports he'd been getting from the radio was about the weather.

Nope, something didn't add up, but the only way he was going to get to the bottom of it was to confront the witch once and for all. All the evidence pointed towards her having some part in it. She lived in the middle of the field where the damn flowers had grown, for heaven's sake. If she hadn't done that herself, she could at least be charged with being an accessory. Perhaps during the interrogation, he would uncover the ringleader of the whole sorry mess. Put an end to the plan before it all went too far.

"Bet that Barnaby is involved somewhere along the line, too," Harry careened through the hem of long grass, bursting into the clearing. Ahead of him was the varnished bread house, an amber glow casting a burning radiance around the perimeter. A pall of smoke rose lazily from the square chimney (made from bloomer loaves).

Harry ditched the Space Hopper, flinging it back into the overgrowth. He wished he had his trebuchet with him, but speed was of the essence and I still hadn't written it back into the story so he could use it. Regardless, he had a back-up weapon. Rooting around his bum-pocket, he pulled out a can of Bug Off spray. Sure, it killed insects on a scale which would please the Pol Pot of the entomology world, but it had also been banned worldwide due to its ability to melt people down to their constituent atoms. The last thing he wanted was to reduce Sally down to a putrid gruel, but if she was behind this madness, then he might have no option. Plus, a tiny part of him wanted to see someone being reduced to a puddle of melted goo, especially after the day he'd had.

Shit, for all he knew, this was an elaborate trap, and sure as eggs is eggs, he was walking right into it. That was something for another day, one for his obituary in the local rag. Harry knew he was the only person who could sort this little mystery out. Even if there are a staggering number of pages left in this book. It's probably just adverts or something; I wouldn't worry your pretty little head about it.

As the whole trap scenario played in his head, Harry froze. He could see that the door was open, the glow pouring from the house and out into the field. Blotting out a section in the middle, was a figure. It was too late for a surprise pincer manoeuvre —an impossibility, considering his inability to split himself in two— he'd had have to go in can blazing. See what the crack was.

"Sally, don't move, it's me, Detective Surge. I know what you're trying to do. It's over," he called out across the sundered stalks and drying grass.

With the spray can held by his side, Harry marched across the desolate field. The closer he got, the more the shape in the doorway morphed. He'd only seen the woman an hour or so ago, and she was of a slight build. A diet consisting of bugs, bark and homegrown peyote was bound to keep your weight down, but the black blob standing tall in the doorway was far larger than Sally could ever be.

A spider of fear ran up Harry's back. Shaking it off and crushing the arachnid under foot, the detective felt a tingling sensation in his guts. Something wasn't right here. Something wasn't right at all. Perhaps it was all the biscuits? Now, only a few feet from the doorway, he froze. "What the…"

Standing just inside the bread hovel, was an Os Furem orchid, though this one was six foot tall. Its thick rotund body supported its weight with ease; giant leaves on other side of the stem looked like arms. One waved at him to acknowledge his presence. The head was bent over, the petals interlaced around something hidden from view. They parted to reveal limp arms and legs, the flower holding the witch's body in its thrall.

"Sally?" Harry ventured, his voice blanched of bass and timbre.

"One and the same, Detective."

Squeezing between the woman, her flower captor, and the jamb, Barnaby stepped onto the welcome mat which was actually fifteen individual welcome mats sewn together, stolen to order from Mercia Avenue. He stopped a few feet from Harry, bowed, and removed his hat at the same time. "*Enchanté.*"

"What are—"

Barnaby pressed a gloved finger over Harry's lips. "Shh, my dear boy. You've played your part, now let me play mine. But first, allow me to showcase your impending demise, thus." He clicked his fingers. Looking over the biscuit courier's shoulder, he could see the flower begin to shake the fortuitously unconscious Sally as if she were an obstinate piggy bank, the woman seemingly intent on clinging to the precious money within. Her limbs, completely devoid of tension, slapped against the thick hide of the giant orchid like a rag doll being mauled by an enthusiastic puppy.

The petals parted enough to let Harry see the witch's mouth split open, the skin ripping down to her ears forming a beaming Chelsea smile. With a substantial portal created, Sally's skull slipped forward and bridged the gap between flower and human heads. The orchid paused for dramatic effect, enhanced by Barnaby's gentle clapping. After the brief respite, the suction increased and the woman's skull and neck were sucked free from their skin wrap and into the flower.

Her shoulders caused a momentary blockage, with the orchid having to waggle its captive to try to get it to slip and slide out of the hole in the woman's face. As one of the arms dislocated, the blockage was freed, and the bones continued their exodus from their one careful owner into the giant plant. As the bottom of the ribcage popped out of the breach, the rest of the transfer picked up pace, and within a few seconds, her filleted arms and legs hung down like rogue pairs of tights on a washing line. The tentacles released their grip, and what remained of the witch slopped to the floor, now nothing more than a squeezy flesh tube filled with shiny dewy mulch where unfortunate organs had been blended. This gloopy cocktail dribbled out of sundered orifices, leaving the rubbery suit floating in a sea of blood and liquefied offal.

"FUCKING HELL! What the…how did…but the goo, look at the

goo!" Harry pointed at the scene.

With its work done, the flower rotated towards the detective, taking lumbering steps forward with its mighty leg leaves. Barnaby rested a hand under Harry's chin. "Don't worry, there's more than enough room for you, too."

Coming to a halt, the flower stretched out its leaves, its bulbous head tipping back as if to howl at the burgeoning moon, but nothing came out as it lacked the ability to vocalise threat in any form. Annoyed, it fell back to what it knew was its biggest strength, and loomed over the detective all menacing-like. Its body was distended, bloated with the witch's bones. The stamen tentacles quivered in anticipation, running over Harry's face as if he were an ice lolly and it was a sweltering hot day.

"If you think I'm going out like that, you've got another fucking think coming." Harry lifted up the can of bug spray, but before he could reduce the flower to compost, a leaf knocked it from his hands.

"It's okay, Detective. It won't matter soon." Barnaby teased his gloves off, finger by finger, and dropped them onto the floor. "I thought you'd be a harder quarry to lure here. I mean, who would actually believe the clues I left behind?"

"That was all you?"

Barnaby took off his jacket and let it slip to the floor. "But of course, dear boy. Did you not question the veracity of the events?"

"The diary seemed a little far-fetched; the cat-tarred chicken thing especially, but it was keeping in tone with everything else that was going on. I've got —well, I *had* until some dickhead forgot about it— a three-quarter scale trebuchet, for fuck's sake, that's not standard police issue weaponry. In case you didn't realise."

"So, Sally, seemingly intent on emulating her clearly fabricated ancestor's plan to steal bones from local villagers and use them to build a house seemed perfectly believable?"

"Maybe not now you've said it out loud, but at the time, well…yeah."

"And the diary pages being written on lined paper and in biro? That's pretty standard for the late seventeenth century?"

"Thing is …"

"Yes?"

"You distracted me with those biscuits, that was a cunning move, even I have to give you that one. Well played, knobhead."

"You're telling me, detective, that the sole reason you're stood near-naked in a harvested field of bone-removing orchids, moments from death, is because you're quite partial to a custard cream?"

"It's not the epitaph most would choose, but it could've been a lot worse. Better that than bananas. Urgh."

Barnaby untied his cravat and placed it atop his discarded clothing, and began to unbutton his shirt. "I'm relieved that I didn't overestimate you, Detective."

Harry balled his fists. "You haven't beaten me just yet; I think you'll find I'm full of surprises. Take this, KASOK," he said, taking a swing, which Barnaby easily ducked, his body seemingly made of liquid, simply folding backwards beneath the blow before bobbing back up again.

"Enough of that." Barnaby clicked his fingers at the plant, which quit slobbering over the detective, linked its leaves through the man's arms and pulled him so his back rested against the stem. Harry tensed his muscles and kicked out, but the plant's hold was firm. Taking some time out from his pre-diatribe, Barnaby ran a hand down the detective's face. "There, much better. I don't mind you being a little irate about your predicament, but really…do you think someone like *you* could challenge my superior intellect? Every step of this little journey of ours, I've had you check and mate. Now, I'll allow you the courtesy of asking the questions you undoubtedly have. It's the least I can do before you die."

"I wouldn't normally bother, but what the fuck did Witchy McWitchface have to do with this? Why did you use her?"

With his shirt unbuttoned, Barnaby let it slip from his arms onto the floor and began to work the fly on his trousers. "It is unfortunate, for she did not serve such a grisly death, but I do so detest loose ends. After all, she saved me, Detective Surge, did you know that? From the place I was in before, she brought me back, though I doubt she even knew it."

Harry looked down at the man in front of him, now down to his Y-fronts. "Are you going to make any fucking sense at all, today? Or perhaps you want to scribble this down and put it in one of your little fortune biscuits—"

"I prefer *clue cookies*, Detective."

"Stop the bullshit express, Barney. It's bad enough what you've done to all these people, some of whom I didn't fully loathe, but don't you dare Americanise the finest food group known to man. Answer me straight, you bastard, Sally saved you from what? Being a demonstrative bellend?"

"Such a potty mouth." Barnaby pulled his underpants down and stood naked before the detective. Instead of genitals, he was completely smooth, like a plastic doll. "Admiring the view?"

Harry smirked. "Well, that explains a lot; no wonder you're such a psycho, you have more in common with my ex-wife than I'd given you credit for. She had a moustache, too." Unable to stop himself, he kicked Barnaby square where his dick should've been, getting nothing more than the slapping sound of foot hitting padded skin.

"Happy now?"

"I'm fucking ecstatic, Captain Plastic," Harry continued to kick the doughy v-section between Barnaby's legs, who was taking it with remarkably good humour. Way more than I would. Balls or no, I wouldn't be too happy with my quarry kicking me where my love spuds should be. Does that make me a worse person? Probably not, because Barnaby is just a character spawned from my imagination, and now, yours. You can consider the logic of that later on, when you have a moment.

"I'm not exactly human, you see, Once, perhaps, but now I'm something which transcends this puny flesh." Barnaby trapped the kicking foot between his thighs and squeezed tight. Content that he was no longer being groin-kneaded, he began to push his fingers into the hollow of his throat. At first, the digits merely depressed the skin, forming a shallow cave which spread across his upper torso. The elasticity —although remarkable— was never going to last; the skin finally split and tore open.

Barnaby reached within the ragged hole, closing his fingers round a zip and tugging it down. As he undid himself, his body began to hiss like a punctured whoopee cushion and the fat physical form of the man began to wilt. As the sallow skin suit hung from the bones within, and with the air now expelled, near skeletal hands untangled the covering from the top down, disrobing the man slowly. In a few seconds, the empty suit flopped to the floor, and a deformed skeleton —save for Barnaby's face— stood in its place. "Da-dah."

"FUCKING HELL."

The collection of bones had a hunched back, bowed legs and ribs which looked more at home trying to hold together a large barrel of aging whiskey. As Barnaby reached for his mask, Harry snapped. "Hold up."

"What is it, Detective?"

"I made a throwaway comment earlier that if this was a Scooby-Doo sort of thing, I'd love to rip your face off to discover who you truly are. Would you mind?" Barnaby gestured to the plant, which relinquished its hold on its captive. "Much obliged." Harry grabbed Barnaby's nose and yanked the face clean off, mightily relieved that only a gleaming skull was underneath and not a genuine human face. That would've been *really* weird.

"Done?"

"Yeah, thanks. Feels like I've kept a promise to someone," Harry said, moving his arm back and allowing the orchid to hold him prisoner once more.

"If you think that's nifty, check this out." Barnaby's bony fingers pressed into the eye socket and scooped out the eyeballs as if they were nothing but blobs of kumquat sorbet and held them out to Harry on the palm of his skeleton hand. "Painted pickled onions, took ages to get the colour just right. I should've been happy with a generic blue, but I wanted grey and green flecks in, you know?"

"There's no fucking way they're pickled onions. You've been stealing from the Eye Orphanage, haven't you? There's low and then there's you, down in the gutter of utter bastardy ...”

Between pointy fingers, Barnaby picked up one of the eyes and shoved it into Harry's gob, pinching his lips shut as it dawned on him that his mouth had been annexed. Harry crunched down on it, and after getting past the outer paint shell, let out an agreeable sound as he found out that they really were pickled onions.

“I told you so. Now. Do you have any actual questions for me, or shall I just get to the bit where I take care of you and move onto the second half of what shall come to pass?”

What the hell is he talking about? Hang on, he's become aware that I'm relating his story to other people. Shit. I better be quiet, or he might give me the other eyeball — I fucking hate pickled onions. Barnaby is right about one thing, though, it is heading into the second act. Bit of a surprise, huh?

What do you mean ‘no’? Sod off back to Soddery then. Honestly. Anyway, for those of you still interested —and now that Barnaby's attention is back to Harry, I'll continue to relay the events.

“At some point, you might actually want to tell me about Sally. You know, like you were going to all those paragraphs ago?”

“Oh bother, you're right. I did promise you some backstory, and I am a man of my word.”

“If you are, would you mind admitting that you're a complete twat and then launch yourself into the local quarry? I'd then be able to take full credit for saving the day and wrapping this up pretty neatly.”

“No.”

“THEN GET THE FUCK ON WITH IT.”

“Very well, but first, Detective Surge, do you not wonder why I chose you?”

“Not really.”

“Because…what? What do you mean, *not really*?”

“It's kinda obvious, really. I'm everything you're not: funny, witty, in possession of an actual body —and a giant knob. What do you have that I don't?”

Barnaby would have loved to have smirked just then; he would have given anything to have given Harry a smile that said FUCK OFF, YOU SMUG BASTARD, in big letters like that. Instead, he used words, uttered aloud so that they could be heard. “Why, my dear boy. I have *you*. That's more than you have.”

“Fine. Come on then, why choose me? I could do with a lift about now.”

“Do you recall attending a traffic accident a few years back on the A303? A late-night collision between a lorry and a low-flying glider? You were first on the scene, if I remember correctly?”

Harry sagged. "I do. Utter carnage, bodies all over the place, that damn lorry was responsible for moving the corpses from the grammar plague pits discovered under the main runway at Middle Wallop."

"And the glider pilot, Detective, do you remember him?"

"Poor fucker never stood a chance; he was air-dropping traffic bollards to warn of imminent roadworks, the damn road was supposed to be clear. Hang on …"

"Yes?"

"The pilot…when I found him, he was clinging onto life halfway up a telegraph pole, naked except for a silky pair of ladies' knickers."

"Go on …"

Harry regarded the skeleton standing in front of him. "He was too high up, so I had to poke him back down to earth with a branch. After he carked it, I managed to check him out properly, without him trying to get me to give him mouth-to-mouth. Urgh. He had a hunchback, legs which looked like he's been riding a horse since conception, and that chest of his…it was as big as a great big fat fucker who loves nothing more than forging diaries, leaving crappy clues in biscuits, painting pickled onion eyes and wearing fat suits."

"Perhaps…you think maybe?"

"It…it was you?

A convenient silence befell the glen. Barnaby clapped his hands together. "Oh no, no, no. In this particular tale, I was just the lowly mortuary assistant working late one night who unzipped a body bag only to find their identical twin who had been hidden from them their entire life. To say it came out of the blue would be understating its impact."

"I bet. Two fat fucks in the same place and time…correction, two fat *ugly* fucks in the same place, both wearing women's underwear, what are the chances?"

"That's not what I meant. The shock…it killed me."

The gaggle of feral children who had ventured to the edge of the clearing were hoping to acquire some more blood. They gasped a collective gasp before scarpering back to their underground boltholes. Harry shrugged. "Ah, well. Win some, lose some. Though what does that have to do with me? I didn't kill your morbidly obese, cross-dressing, identical twin brother, did I?"

Moving in close, Barnaby's teeth chattered mere inches from Harry's face. "No, you didn't. But it was you who removed all his interior organs and replaced them with IOUs and chunks of asphalt so you could sell them on the black market."

"Ah …"

"Not just that. You had taken a number of the shrivelled-up plague victims and shoved them up his bottom before sewing the cheeks together to try and keep your secret safe from prying eyes."

"I did do that. Yes. I was bored, you know? I'd called the accident in, but with it being early morning, and everyone already either being dead for centuries or a few minutes, no-one was in a huge rush. I thought *why not?* If it's any consolation, he was the first one in my collection. That photo is pride of place on the 'people with the things I've shoved up their arsehole' wall back home."

"You besmirched my only brother. I swore an oath to get revenge upon the person who had fouled him in such a manner. His pestilent body had to be loaded into a submersible and fired into the inky depths of the Mariana Trench to ensure that it would not taint the land."

"That's the basis for a decent horror story there; you should tell Todd. You know. If he lives."

"I might just do that, detective."

"Hang on a minute, pal, I thought you'd carked it? How the fuck do you know all about this if you were already sparko on the floor playing 'Dead Twin 101, The Next Level: Death', Hmm?"

"I'm so glad you asked. My funeral was a muted affair, I had but two attendees, and one of those was responsible for dragging the budget cardboard coffin into the hole in the ground."

"Aww, diddums. Who was the other one?"

Barnaby patted the flower stem behind Harry. "Dear Sally. It would seem that it was her custom to pay tribute to those poor souls who have no-one to mourn them, for the cemetery is just over yonder beyond those trees. As my coffin was upended into what should've been my final resting place, a stiff breeze blew the flimsy lid up-up and away. She cast a solitary flower upon my broad chest, one that had bloomed that very morn outside a house made of varnished bread."

"This is all awfully convenient, eh?"

Continuing to stroke the plant nuzzled against his hand, Barnaby replied, "Quite. A relative of this rare orchid was pressed against my bosom as the frigid soil was shovelled over my lifeless body, imprisoning me within an earthy tomb. Held tight six-foot under, and sensing that which it desires, the flower stirred from its timeless slumber. Affixing itself to my corpulent lips, it removed one solitary piece of me." Barnaby held his arm in front of Harry, the left radius missing.

"I *thought* you were a bit limp-wristed."

"After it worked its way free from our shared grave, it returned to stir one of its larger brethren from its fugue - a magnificent specimen just like this. It trekked the short distance to my burial site, burrowed down to my body, and ingested me —much like it did with Sally. Once I had been exhumed, and under a full moon—"

"Fucking hell, horror trope number seventy-four, come in, please."

"—the flower birthed me upon this very field. As I lay under that pregnant moon, I howled unto the sky that vengeance would be mine. I had been given the chance at another life, and I would not waste it. I hurried to the local charity shops, scavenged a second-hand body suit, and after some amendments so it would fit my exacting form—"

"Great big fatty boom-boom."

"—I returned to the place of my rebirth. Changed, but whole. More than I'd ever been. Using my brother's life insurance, I bought both the witch's silence and her land. Since that night, the flowers had awoken and I used this fertile ground to grow them in droves, preparing them for the day I would unleash them upon you unsuspecting fools and I could reveal my true intentions."

"Which are? And please, bear in mind that this has been going on for ages now, so could you please get to the fucking point?"

Barnaby leant in so close that Harry's nose disappeared into the skeleton's nasal cavity. "I'm taking it all, Detective Surge."

"Ha ha ha ha ha ha ha ha ha ha ha ha ha ha ha ha ha. That's fucking priceless. What are you taking, exactly? People's arm bones? Big fucking deal, they've got two, you know? Gonna go and build a stupid little bone house like the one in your piece of fiction?"

Right on cue —which is pretty fucking coincidental if you ask me— orchid number one bounded through the edge of the tall grass, bouncing like an organic pogo stick. It came to a halt behind Barnaby, who slowly moved to one side. "Oh no, Detective Surge, I'm most certainly not building a house, I'm making something else entirely. You see, the flower which took that first bone of mine did not keep it for itself. They have a rather unusual ability I'd like to share with you. Regard."

The flower reared backwards, the nub of freshly-procured bone visible briefly when illuminated by the moonlight. Aww, poetic, eh? It jabbed it into the ground and made a noise like a cat having found a hitherto difficult-to-reach place to bring up a furball. The head began to sink into the stem itself, the petals breaking off and fluttering to the ground. As the flower retracted into itself, it forced the bone deeper into the earth. When it was nothing but an inch of green mulch, the flower fizzled away into sludge.

"Ooh, the flower had a shit. What a rush."

Barnaby pointed. "I read what you said earlier about Latin, detective, and you're quite right, it is a dead language. As such, I've dispensed with the Os Furem moniker and, much like Clue Cookies™, I have bestowed upon them a name more befitting of their special powers. Detective, let me introduce you to…the Harryhausen Orchid."

As the green goo fizzed on the surface of the scoured earth, the soil began to bubble and foam as if suffering a reaction to the invader within its brown midst. A skeletal hand rose from the frigid ground, slapping against the cold sod. Like a crane, it hauled its body out, anatomically the same as a human being, but exactly four feet and two inches tall. Shaking the dirt from its body, it stood to attention behind Barnaby, creator and createe staring at a rather bemused detective. "Behold…humanity's damnation."

"It's a bit…"

"What? Small? I know, I'm not sure why it does that. I concede that it does diminish the appearance of threat."

"No. I didn't mean that."

"What, then?"

"It's a bit shit. Is this honestly your plan? Rustle up some really crappy dumpy little skeletons? What are you going to do, take over Tiny Town?"

Barnaby put his hands on his bony hips. "In mere hours, the scene here will be repeated in towns and villages up and down the country. In weeks, across the entire world. Nothing and no-one can stop me. Least of all …you." He clicked his fingers, and the flower head opened, the stamen tentacles latching onto the side of Harry's head.

"No. Wait," Harry's voice echoed down the orchid's throat/stem thing.

Barnaby held up a hand. "What is it?"

"You're a complete dick, and your plan is shitter than the time I used your brother's ear canal as a temporary toilet."

"I'm going to miss you, Detective Surge."

"Really? I'm not surprised, I'm the best."

"I was being sarcastic; I'm going to miss you as much as I miss defecating. Now, I have an entire world to bend to my whim, and you? You get to die. Goodbye." With another click of his fingers, the plant closed around Harry's head and sucked until every single bone was inside its body, before depositing the empty condom of skin onto the ground.

Barnaby clapped his hands together. "Why, I do believe I just made a rap."

Chapter
Sixteen

Malva sylvestris

"No, Sonic, get off me. Get off. Leave my leg alone. Stop trying to pull my skids down. No, please, don't clamber inside my—" Chaz sat up quickly, his addled mind hoping that the speedy blue hedgehog was just an avatar from a terrifying nightmare, and wasn't really trying to climb inside him and beat the record time for running around stage one of his lower intestines.

Thirty-one point eight-five seconds, if you're interested.

The hospital room came back into focus, helped in no small part by Chaz blinking rapidly and rubbing his eyes. Funny, that. The curtains had been pulled across but didn't meet in the middle, letting some light streak in through the rather grimy windows. As he looked round the room, motes of dust —which had been coating him rather effectively— - began to float back down, having been puffed upwards from their resting place. Chaz looked down at the bed and saw that he had been well and truly tucked in. The outline of his legs was prominent, although on closer inspection they appeared misshapen. His left leg looked a bit thinner, but it was his right one that seemed odd, puffed up, as if it had been over-inflated and abandoned. Hijinks gone awry.

It was around this point that his fuzzy brain noted he had three such appendages. Between the two usual legs, he had another lengthy bulge, complete with knee. Fumbling with the end of the blankets, his feeble fingers struggled to get some leverage over the taut edge. Whoever had left him like this knew their stuff; he guessed it was his nan, as she was notorious for tucking him up at night as a kid, and him losing circulation from the neck down until the next morning when his grandad would rescue him.

Managing to loosen a corner from the side of the mattress, his fingers pawed at the itchy covers until he finally pulled them free. "What the?" There they were. Three legs. He doubted himself; perhaps this was one of Sonic's plans, try to confuse him, then dash up his poo-chute when he wasn't prepared, ready to loop-the-loop round his gut piping.

The room began to feel like it was closing in; Chaz could feel his heartbeat punching his inner throat. He had to get out of there. Now. Regardless of the potential danger he faced. For all he knew, the gown he was wearing was one of those ones which tied at the back. He feared that in the gap between the cloth, a crude arrow had been scrawled in blue marker pen, pointing towards his hairy hinterland.

He managed to slide his left leg off the bed, though the damn thing was a dead weight. It was like he'd been sat on the toilet for too long, trying to run a macro on his spreadsheet detailing his misfortune, attempting to unlock the algorithm that would allow him some control over the bad luck that plagued him each and every day.

With the one good leg sorted, he was now faced with a quandary. Which of the two remaining legs was the proper one? For reasons unknown, the one in the middle looked the leggiest, but it felt flaccid. Yet the right one didn't seem to respond to any mental commands. Cupping his hands beneath them both, he lifted them up and over the end of the bed and let them all flop towards the floor. There was only one way to sort this out; stand or sink. Chaz took a few deep breaths in and out before pitching himself forward, eager to discover which of the three apparent limbs would rise to the occasion and take his weight, showing their master which was up to the challenge of transporting him from A to B, maybe even a cheeky stopover at C. He pulled out the tubing from his arm, which snaked to empty pinched plastic bags of ex-sustenance and tried to stand up.

The pain of his face meeting the floor was not wholly unexpected, but it was an unwelcome visitor. As his fingers —which felt like he was in charge of fat sausages— tried to pick up a tooth that had snapped off at the end of his brief journey, he cursed his optimism. Knowing that he wouldn't be able to do much with the tooth even if he could grip it between thumb and forefinger, Chaz rolled onto his back and pulled himself up so that he rested against the bed.

His sudden rise and even more sudden fall had taken it out of him. He felt like he'd been at the gym for at least twelve minutes. It was no good; he *had* to know what the hell had happened to the lower part of his body. Checking that he was hidden from view through the window, and the door was well and truly closed, he began to pull his loose trousers down.

"Is that my knob?"

Pretty much the standard question most people would ask if they awoke to discover that their penis had been replaced by a leg. "Hang on, that's *my* leg," he said, which is good, as there's nothing worse than having someone else's leg replacing your penis. Chaz grunted and managed to flex his middle leg. With one half of the mystery worked out, he diverted all attention and thinking power to the final conundrum. "If that's my leg, then what is this? A spare?"

He poked and prodded it, even going so far as to lean as far forward as he could and give it a bit of a sniff. Nothing untoward. There was a general ambiance of old sweat and dried shit going on, but he had bigger fish to fry —metaphorically speaking— than worry about the stench. Pulling back, he noticed that the new right leg was completely shorn of hair. Poking it made it rustle, and it was at this juncture that he realised it looked like a giant bolster pillow, just considerably less comfortable.

This new limb was pretty shit, if he was being honest. Chaz rested his head against the bed, closed his eyes, and tried to recall the last thing he could remember. Perhaps he had volunteered to be the sole participant in a three-legged race for charity? Had he been press-ganged into a scientific experiment; an attempt to create the first member in a super-race of three-legged people? Could be. It was evident he was in some kind of recovery room, and given the general state of disrepair, the lack of electricity and the poor cleaning routine, it didn't look like a hospital that was in use.

Perhaps…and this was a long shot…Perhaps he'd been kidnapped by a busty mad scientist? Yeah. One who had been carrying out sexy experiments on him. Dressed in skimpy lingerie. Chaz felt right leg number two stir from its slumber, solidifying and beginning to point towards the ceiling. It was at this juncture Chaz noticed two important details about his so-called new limb, bestowed on him by a scantily-clad nymphomaniac. It didn't have a foot, and the end was dome shaped.

"Is *that* my knob? What's it doing there? And why is it so big?"

Well, this was quite the conundrum, but in fairness, he wasn't a medical professional, and these things are always going to be a little overwhelming at first. Regardless of his new arrangement, Chaz had to get up and work out what the hell was going on, weird penis or not. Grabbing hold of the bedside table, he managed to haul himself up to standing, even if he was a bit wobbly. Erect —in both senses of the word— Chaz reached for a convenient pair of crutches and lurched towards the door.

"Hello?" His voice echoed down the corridor, which was in a similar state to the room he'd woken up in. Beds were pushed against the wall, and unravelled bandages stained brown littered the floor like snake skins. Looking up at the signage, he turned towards the Exit sign and began to make his way slowly down the filthy aisle. "Is anyone there?"

Every once in a while, he'd stop to peek into other rooms, all of which were bereft of patients, or medical staff for that matter. Instead, he found the droppings of civilisation. Handbags, watches, items of clothing, and opinions by the bucketload. As he picked up a polo neck jumper with one of the crutches, he heard a noise from behind him, back in the bowels of the building.

He let the jumper slip off the end of the prong onto the floor, slowly turning towards the sound. The noise had a doppelganger join in, both seemingly trying to outdo the other. Before a third joined in, and a fourth. Chaz gulped, or tried to, but saliva production was seemingly low on his body's priority list of getting fired up. He began to edge away from the noise, which was growing louder and louder. He heard a crunch as one crutch speared a glass vial behind him. Chaz was so preoccupied with the burgeoning din that he didn't even yelp as he stepped on the shards of broken glass, still dumbly edging back down the hallway.

Then. He saw them. The origin of the sound. A pack of dogs, all shapes, sizes and breeds, they blocked out the end of the corridor with their bodies. Even from a distance he could see their heads bob up and down in time with their incessant barking. The sound congealed into a violent aria, a wall of yips and growls that no tenor or beatboxer could hope to emulate.

The time to flee was now. But his crappy atrophied body was ill-prepared for such an eventuality. As he lurched to the side, he let his foot-wang hang down as the glass pressed deeper into the soft pads of his feet. Great, *now* he noticed the glass, what an idiot. Knowing it was futile —but aware that if anyone found his decomposing body in the future, he wanted to make it look like he'd at least tried to flee— Chaz began to fling himself down the hall as fast as he could.

He barely got to the next junction, which led to 'Child Dislodgings' and 'Soul Impaction' before the first hound caught up with him. For the second time since his awakening, his face met with the floor, and, crutches discarded, he slid down the mucky lino nose-first, coming to a rest with his forehead touching a soiled bedpan. Dog tongue lolled over his assortment of lower limbs; it was a little perturbing in places. Turning over to face his doom, he gritted his teeth, and braced for death.

"Sadie, get off him," a voice commanded.

The licking ceased, as did the doggy choir, eager feet pitter-pattering back to their master. Daring to open his eyes, Chaz looked up into the face of a man with a shaggy beard, his upper brow stained white with lumpy curds nestled in the wiry thatch. A hand reached down to him. "Hello there, I'm Venkatesh Singh, welcome to Doggoland."

Chapter
Seventeen

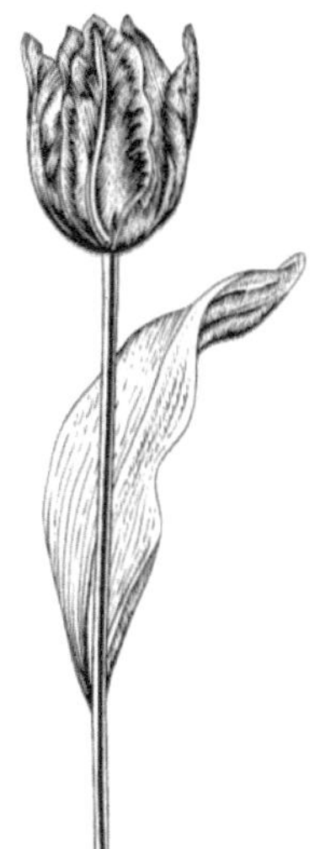

Tulipa

It had barely been a minute since Chaz had been deposited on a sofa in Doggoland when his mysterious saviour had picked up the nearest canine, placed it on his lap, and began to tug at its nipples, the milk squirting noisily into a metal bowl usually reserved for collecting human kidneys. He tried to cajole some small talk out of the canine dairy farmer. "How long…how long have I been…you know?"

Singh chuckled and carried on milking the dachshund. "Three weeks. Or twenty-one days. How does five-hundred-and thirty-two-hours sound? Give or take. You should be grateful, though. I didn't forget you like everyone else did. Not me. I kept your feeding tubes full for the first few weeks before I figured it would be of more use to my doggos. You gotta remember that everyone thought you were a goner, especially when they couldn't revive you after stage one of your operation. Although by then, anyone that could've helped you had far more pressing things to deal with."

"Like what?"

The man stopped milking the dog and shook his right arm at Chaz, which wobbled on weakened moorings. "Like those bone-stealing flowers, of course. Where the hell have you been? In a coma or something?"

"Well, yeah."

"Course. Silly me." Venkatesh quit the weird shaking of his arm and got back to the main order of business. As the milk jetted out of the dog's nipple it splashed off the inside of the bowl and sprayed both the man and the floor around him.

"Things must be bad out there," Chaz massaged his legs; anything to distract him from the milking process.

"What do you mean?"

"Well, look at you. You're holed up in this place, evidently little food or water, having to resort to milking feral animals as your only source of sustenance. Whatever happened, it must've been terrible."

Venkatesh stopped mid-stream and the dachshund yelped, unsatisfied. "Oh no, things out there aren't too bad. Probably. I haven't been out since I woke up one bone less. I like it here. I can live out my wildest dreams and fantasies."

Chaz sat up slowly, trying to work out where the closest door was, and whether he could get to it without being rugby tackled or mauled by any one of the large pack of dogs that were lounging around what used to be the waiting room. "Erm…look, if you let me go, I won't tell anyone what you're doing here, okay? This is all rather overwhelming, bone-stealing flowers, dog milk…my anatomy. How about you just shove me in a wheelchair and push me out of the doors, I won't tell another living soul what you're doing here, your secret's safe with me."

"And what's my secret, exactly?" Singh was still mid-squeeze, milk-flecked fingers working the dog's nipples.

"You know…your weird things. The dogs and that. Different strokes for different folks, I'm not judging." Chaz said the words fully in the knowledge that it's impossible - having just come out of a coma, and having an elongated knob - not to judge someone who is milking a dog right in front of you.

Finishing off the squeeze, the dog let out a relieved yip before Singh placed it on the floor, patted its head and watched as it padded off to a cushion to have a bit of a snooze. Swirling the milk around the bowl, he let it settle before leaning over it and taking in a massive sniff. His head fell backwards and the words that come out of his mouth sounded like they were from a completely different person. "You're not a fan of my life choices, then?"

Chaz pointed at the bleedin' obvious. "The dog milk sniffing. It's not really normal, is it?"

"Define normal in a world gone mad."

"Eh?"

"Draw the baseline in a civilisation where everything has changed irrevocably."

"Have you had a mental breakdown? I can't say I'm getting much from you except for weird riddles and the nagging sense that I'm experiencing the last few minutes of my life."

Singh took another big sniff before setting the bowl on the chair next to him, eyes glazed, pupils straining to burst out of their borders and into the white bit. "I wouldn't kill you."

Chaz wiped his brow. "Phew, that's a relief."

"I'd only do that in your sleep or if you tried to leave me. You can't leave me. Not now. I've got a new friend. Best friends forever, what do you say?"

"Maybe?"

Singh slid to the edge of the chair, slipping a scalpel out from a hidden pocket sewn into his inner sleeve. "The paramedics…they told me things. Things you can do to a person to stop them walking out on you," he said, slashing the air from left to right.

"FFFTTT, slice through the Achilles tendon, you won't be going anywhere then. Perhaps…perhaps I could solve science's greatest puzzle and get *you* to produce milk? I could carry out experiments to give you great big udders. I've got all the time in the world, especially after what happened."

"And what was that, exactly? Please, tell me. I've got nothing here. Last thing I remember was…oh god…Natasha! I have to go find her!" Chaz fumbled for his crutches, disturbing a pair of border collies who were staring off into middle space.

Venkatesh laughed and slumped back into the chair. "It's too late, my friend. You're way too late."

"What…what have you done to her?"

"Me? Nothing. She's just like all the others." Singh sat back up again, staring at Chaz. "Gone. They're all gone." He began to wave the scalpel in the air, trying to spell out his name in cursive.

Chaz gripped the handle of the crutches —with luck, and the right wind conditions, he figured he could snap forward and take a swing at the crazed man. "Where? Where have they gone?"

Holding the surgical implement like a laser pointer, he swished his hand, before pointing at the main doors. They had been chained closed and a pile of furniture had been stacked up against them. An Alsatian sat on top of the lot, its milk glands swollen and sore. "Gone. They left."

"Oh, they just…left?"

"Well yeah, duh. Why would they stay here? When you wake up with one bone missing, what are you going to do? Stick around for the top-notch food? See if those damn flowers want to come back for seconds? Not on your nelly. No, the ones who woke up first had the right idea alright, they got first dibs on all the cool stuff. Unlike me."

"What happened to you?"

"We weren't incapacitated at the beginning; we still had all our bones when the first ones woke up. I read a newspaper a few days after the first lot had gone, you know, when I came to in this state. They called us the *second wave*, more like the *stupid* wave if you ask me. When the first lot woke up, we tried to stop them smashing open the vending machines, stealing the drugs, looting the stationary cupboard. Stupid sods left all the doors open; we didn't even see *them* until it was too late."

"See who?"

Singh pointed to the wall behind Chaz. There, impaled by an epidural syringe, was a wilting flower. You know the ones, don't you? "Them. They were upon us before we had a chance. So small, so nimble, so unexpected. I saw Nurse Sandra get taken out by one outside of the 'Paper Cut' department. I remember turning to run for it, then WHOOM, blackness. I woke up on the floor a few hours later; it was dark, sirens blaring, people screaming, shouting. My arm felt heavy and limp and that's when I saw they'd taken my bone too. After that? Those I couldn't scare off, I knocked out with a homemade blowpipe and some strong sedative. Dragged them outside along with any others who had one of those flowers on them. Sealed the place up. That's how I stayed until the first one of my doggo friends showed up," The ex-doctor said, stroking the dachshund.

"They just appeared?"

"Yeah. A few at first. I ignored them to begin with. Was working out the best way I could end it all. But how can you ignore *them*? Smashed in one of the lower windows in the main door and they came bounding in. Something must've drawn them here. Who knows what?"

It's at this juncture I feel it's important that I mention a series of cave paintings outside of Barnsley. Many assert that they were done by humans, but they failed to acknowledge the delicate paw-work that went into the images of a hospital and a solitary lunatic within. Etched above, a single word: *Dogtopia.* If you're a proper canine enthusiast you'll already know all about this, though, so I feel silly for mentioning it. I'd also like to have it put on record that I am *not* paid a fee by the company that runs the exhibit to advertise the quite spectacular work I've just mentioned. I'm not some corporate shill out to make a few quid and blow it on exotic *art pamphlets.*

Though…if you're after the best dog cave paintings this side of Ontario, then you really should visit the Barnsley Caves of Whimsy. Located just off junction thirty-seven of the M1. As they say, it'd be a *terrier*ble shame if you missed it.

Chaz looked around; for all of Singh's quirks, and it was clear he had many, the dogs themselves seemed happy enough. "What's the world like…out there?"

Singh shrugged. "Don't know. Don't care. The screaming stopped pretty early on; it all sounds pretty normal if I'm being honest. But I'm good in here, and now I've got you, well, I can finish up your surgery and we can form a dynamic duo. Just me, you and the dogs. It'll be heaven."

"Finish up my surgery?"

"Well yeah, Steve."

"Who's Steve?"

"Duh, you are, dummy."

"That's not my name. It's Chaz, and if you insist on calling me that, you're just going to confuse people. Okay?"

Venkatesh paused to contemplate his life choices, before he slowly nodded. "Fine, I thought it would've been a fun little thing to do. Ya know, call you Steve all the time."

"Well it isn't, and now someone is going to have to remove this so-called joke from this point on. Do you realise how much unnecessary work you've caused?"

Venkatesh shook his head, completing the second part of head-moving-adjective bingo. "I thought it was funny."

"Let's just forget it happened and move on…bugger, what's my line again?"

(Hang on, I'll just hold up this sign).

Squinting, Chaz read from a hastily scrawled piece of cardboard. "So, what do you mean by *finishing up my surgery*?"

Venkatesh sidled up to his new BFF, plonked himself down, and rested a hand on Chaz's new leg. "What do you think I mean? I'll wager that you've discovered that the pipework switcheroo of your little *extension* hasn't taken place yet. You want that sorted out, don't you?"

Chaz pushed the hand from his penis-leg. "I didn't even want this done to me in the first place."

"Course you didn't. Your problem was that because you were passed out when they brought you in, the ten-minute rule takes effect."

"Ten-minute rule?"

Singh picked up a scruffy terrier and started to scratch under its chin. "Yeah, if you don't wake up within ten minutes of being brought in, then someone calls dibs on what they get to do to you. With your new girlfriend unconscious, Carl figured he'd help you out and turn your member into something that would trouble tailors everywhere."

"That doesn't sound very ethical."

"Maybe not, but it is funny. Anyway, if the flowers hadn't come by and ruined anything, you'd have been thanking him."

"No I wouldn't, look at it. It's a deformity, how can I live life normally now?"

"I dunno, use the cubicle instead of the urinal? Look, it doesn't matter, it's just you and me now. You can let it all hang out for all I care; I won't judge you or feel inferior."

Chaz stood up, half-naked, hands on crutches. "There is no way I'm staying here. I've got to get out there, find out what happened to my family, Natasha, everybody. Sorry to tell you this, but you're a loon and you scare me. There, I said it."

After a brief and thoroughly awkward pause, Singh sighed. "Fine. But can I ask a favour?"

"What?"

Venkatesh waved the blade around. "Can I have your bone?"

"No."

"Go on, give it to me! It's the least you can do after I kept you alive."

"No way. This is the first time in my life that *I'm* the lucky one."

"That's right, rub it in, why don't you? Insensitive sod."

"Don't you want to get out of this place? Go home, see the people you care about? Got to do something other than stay in here relieving dogs of their milky goodness."

"They're my family now," Singh said, signalling the entire pack of dogs with his non knife-wielding arm, "what more could I ask for?"

"Well, I need more. Perhaps if I could get to the bottom of what's happened, maybe I could do something about it? I can't get everyone's bones back, but I can try to stop the madman or woman that did this."

Careful not to disturb the bowl of milk, which still had some good pulls left on it before he'd need to refill for another hit, Venkatesh reached behind the row of chairs. "Here, if you're dead set on abandoning me, and trying to get to the bottom of all of this, you might need these." He pulled out a wad of yellowing paper and held it out.

"What's that?"

"The Detective who tried to stop this before, and a *great* job he did of that too, I should add, was collecting these…fortune biscuits, I guess you could call them."

"CLUE COOKIES!" Barnaby shouted from a completely different part of the book.

The pair carried on as if they hadn't heard it, because they hadn't. They're characters, you see, and only I choose what they are and aren't aware of.

Chaz thumbed through the sheets of paper, trying desperately to get up to speed with developments so that we wouldn't have to waste too much time explaining shit all over again. "Hmm, these came from biscuits?"

"Yep, this guy in a top hat and tails used to hand them out every time someone was afflicted by the flowers. Bound to have something to do with it."

"That's a strange plot device."

"What're you gonna do?"

"All kinds of biscuits, you say?"

"You name it, we ate them. Got to the stage where we were running out of types of biscuit, if I'm being honest with you."

"Even cookies, then?"

"Yep, milk chocolate and hazelnut, if I remember correctly."

"Clues in cookies, so I guess you could say that these were—"

Venkatesh threw the scalpel at Chaz, lopping off a part of his ear lobe. "Oh no you don't. We're British, we won't have any Americanisation here. They're fortune biscuits. I'll allow destiny delights at a push, but nothing else."

Barnaby curled over the top of the page and bellowed, "CLUE COOKIES, YOU FOOLS!"

Staunching the blood with the sleeve of his gown, Chaz picked through the sheaves of hints. "They make mention of a Clagton, I wonder where that is? I suppose I could sneak down to the library and see if I can figure it out."

"No can do," Venkatesh said, patting the head of a golden retriever who had retrieved the scalpel, because they're good like that. Perhaps we should call them scalpel retrievers? Just a thought.

"Why not? It's the perfect place to start."

"It's not time to go back there yet; there's a big important scene coming up later in the library, would be silly to go there now, it'd ruin the impact."

"Right…so any idea where I should start?"

"I heard the rubbish policeman mention Mercia Avenue. If you were to visit that place, it would really help set things up as we spiral towards the lacklustre finale."

"Okay, but I think I might just pop back home first, try and find something more fitting."

Venkatesh shook his head. "I'm afraid you can't do that."

"Why not?"

"You can only go to one of six places; we can't be introducing anywhere new at this point; it'd ruin the joke."

"Whose joke?"

Singh shrugged. "Just some weirdo." He rooted around in his special item alcove and pulled out the world's largest ball of yarn, which easily beat the one from Tucson. Easily. He dug around to find the end. "Go on then, come here a minute."

"What are you going to do?"

"I'm going to do what you ask of me and let you leave."

"That's very decent of you."

"But once you've fixed it all, I want you to come back to me, so I'm going to tie this to your actual leg. That way, when you've saved us all, you can tug on the line seventeen times and I'll reel you in."

"Is that going to work?"

"Of course it is, I just said so. Plus, if you die, I can drag your lifeless body back here to feed my dogs."

"You're all heart."

Holding the red wool up, Singh beckoned Chaz closer. "Look, there are two ways out of Doggoland, Chaz: with this tied round your ankle, or off the roof as I keep throwing you to your eventual death. It's only one-storey, you see, so I'll have to hurl you off a few times before you die. Now I don't really care which, just make your mind up because it's rottweiler milk sniffing time, which is fast becoming the new highlight of my week."

Chapter
Eighteen

Delphinium elatum

To save his modesty, and to stop the end of his massive dong-leg getting too dirty, or bits of grit getting caught under the foreskin, Chaz had covered the tip in a bin bag and had requisitioned a blanket as an itchy sarong. It'd have to do for now; better-fitting clothes or a penis-reduction would be more beneficial, but time was one thing he did not have on his side.

The main thing was that he didn't know what the hell waited outside for him in the real world; by now an undoubted dystopia full of pitfalls and perils of impossible design. It then came as a shock when he left the hospital — hiding in a conveniently placed bush to observe proceedings— and saw that the world seemed so very normal.

Cars still drove on roads, birds still flew in the sky, and people still strolled down the pavements, all at a nice sedate pace and giving no clues at all to the casual observer that anyone was in danger.

In a way, Chaz was a little disappointed. For so long his life had been one disaster after another, that one of his secret desires was for the world to go to shit and for everyone else to get a taste of bad luck for once. Yet, here he was, with doomsday seemingly having been given a three-week head-start, and it looked like any other day.

Still, appearances can be deceiving, and knowing enough about bad luck to last him a lifetime, he decided it would make sense to stick to shrubberies and grass verges. If he could cross the road, he could sneak through an abandoned cemetery (which now doubled up as a nuclear waste dumping ground) and take a shortcut to Charlton itself. He just had to avoid detection by the legendary family that lived in the hallowed glowing wasteland —the one that would capture, torture and eventually turn into a stuffed animal, anyone that dared cross their estate– lest his little trip be over before it even got started.

What would be the chances of that happening?

With his luck?

He took another look at the apparently ordinary scene that was playing out down the main road. Everyone looked so normal, except for the absence of one of their arms, at least. But perhaps that was the problem. Maybe…these flowers, when they stole the bones, they messed with something inside of the victim's head? Singh was quite clearly insane, but was it through enforced isolation, lack of vitamins and being hopped-up on sniffing dog milk, or was it something else? Something unseen?

Chaz remembered a film he'd watched as a kid, Invasion of the Body Snatchers. The aliens in that looked like normal people, but they weren't, they were evil pod people. Who's to say that if he strolled on down the tarmac, bidding good morning to Mr & Mrs Normal, they weren't going to turn into rabid psychopaths, rip his head off, and drop-kick it to their friends on the other side of the road?

Hmm. This was a tricky one. His choice was either a quick nip through the irradiated, and, highly likely haunted lands of the notorious Richardson family of deranged mutants, or run the gauntlet of potential pod people and all that that entails. "Better the devil you know," Chaz deduced, and waited for a lull in both traffic and pedestrians before gathering his knob-leg under one arm and sprinting across the road, clambering over the rusting chain link fence of the village's resident inbreds.

Taking care to neither succumb to the charming wiles of the succubi that sat atop the gravestones, nor dip his wang-leg-peg into a puddle of radioactive goo, Chaz picked a tentative path through the glowing green lands of pure unadulterated nightmare fuel. The things he'd seen already …

He passed a boyband practising their harmonies pretty much as soon as he had vaulted the decrepit boundary. Their severed heads had been sewn onto the bodies of seven-legged squirrels. They had a fearsome visage, though their off-key wailing was easily the worst part. Chaz had to fight every instinct he possessed that told him to cave their heads in with a chunk of iridescent graphite.

A little further in came the worst sight to befall human eyes. It was a man, resplendent of beard, wearing chinos that were too short *and* too tight, sporting boat shoes with NO FUCKING SOCKS ON. AARRRRGGGGHHHH, the humanity. Where is your god now!?

Beyond that, and with the tendrils of insanity seeping in through his very pores, he saw the dilapidated house where the Richardsons lived. From within, he could hear the strains of local radio playing. The animals. As in, the family were animals for listening to local radio, not the band, The Animals.

Chaz knew this next stage had to be done just right, any wrong movement, any accidental clangs, bangs, whistles or yelps, and his location would be compromised. In no time at all, he would be the centre of attention in a game of *I can make this one's head go all the way round*. That's a game you only play once, on account of death or paralysis from your spinal column splintering into at least three separate pieces.

He checked the path ahead, mapping it out mentally so he didn't stray too close to anything which his bad luck could amplify and completely ruin his day. After stepping over the gaping toothy jaws of a miniature bear trap - which had grown eyes and a pair of noses - Chaz prepared himself for what would come next. Making sure he had enough slack on the woollen twine that trailed behind him, he rose from his haunches and went to dash.

Before his muscles could propel him forwards, he saw a flash off to his right. He ducked down quickly, careful not to teeter backwards into the waiting gob of the bear trap, which also had a tongue that was licking the air. "Go on, let me bite you," it lisped.

"No, shut up."

"Nibble your nuts a little bit?"

"Shhh, leave me alone."

"How about I just clamp down softly onto your dimpled buttock so I can savour human flesh one more time?"

"Not a chance, now please, keep it down."

The bear trap rolled its eyes. "All the bloody same, you lot, don't want me to slam around your ankle and slurp on your lovely warm blood. Do you know what it's like for a sentient bear trap out here?"

"They'll hear you if you don't zip it," Chaz said, making a viewing hole through the thicket he was currently ducked down in. He could hear a steady *click-clack-click-clack* from the path beyond. He did a double take at the talking trap. "Besides, aren't you a little small to be a bear trap? Look more like a ferret trap."

"How bloody dare you. Size isn't everything, you know. It's not my fault that I didn't get as much of the special glowing compost as poor old Ralph over there." The diminutive ferret/bear trap pointed its two noses at a shovel sticking out of a small pond of glowing bubbling green liquid opposite. The handle disappeared into the low-hanging clouds which were threatening a pesky downpour. "Lucky sod got absolutely soaked in the stuff. It's on my bucket list to be that big."

"What do you know about dreams and ambitions?"

"More than you'd know. Rest assured that one of these days…I'm gonna tick off my two remaining items."

"If I ask you what they are, will you shut up?"

"Hmmm, no, but I'll tell you what the other one is. I'm going to find myself an unsuspecting person, crack open their head and go swimming inside their skull, chomping all the squishy bits down into a fine syrup. Mmmm."

"That's disgusting."

"Hey, everyone's got to eat, you know. Anyway, look at you, knocking about with your three legs. Surely you wouldn't begrudge a famished deformed bear trap noshing down on your spare one?"

Chaz flashed the end of his penis-leg off to the trap, whose eyes widened in shock. "There, see. It's not a leg, and there's no way I'm letting you take a chunk out of it."

"Fair play, guv. Don't think I'd be too comfortable getting my teeth into that anyway. I bid you good day. Honestly…people say *I'm* weird for being spawned in this radioactive cesspit, you're something else entirely."

With the brief diversion out of the way, Chaz focused on the sound, which was getting louder and louder. When they came into view, he had to shove a hand over his mouth to stop from screaming. Running up the path were ten midget skeletons, all in perfect lockstep. Coming to a standstill outside the knackered building, they lined up facing the front door. One from the end broke rank and marched forwards, stopping only to smack its hand on the front door. "Open up," It demanded, getting little response except curtains twitching from the front-facing rooms.

The skeleton continued to pound on the door, which began to whine against the onslaught, ancient hinges at the edge of their limit. "We know you're in there, open up or we'll be forced to break the door down."

This was bad. Of all the available doomsday scenarios Chaz had imagined, dwarven skeletons were a thing his brain had not even considered. Pod people, yes. Invisible radioactive dinosaurs, a possibility. But vicious-looking, fully articulated, fifty-inch-tall skeletons? Pah! Who would even think this shit up?

(Leave your sarcastic comments where they are.)

As the door creaked, the top hinge gave way and the door sunk inwards, revealing the father of the Richardson clan, Richard. "What do you want? This is private property," He delivered the words as if he'd spent his entire life dealing with the bony innards of people knocking on his front door with unknown demands. Mind you, living where they lived, and with the vast spectrum of mutated creatures and electrical appliances that laid siege to their domicile every few months, skeletons were probably a blessed relief.

The skeleton at the door did nothing except point back to a rusting Land Rover that was sat on the drive. Its tyres were bald, a few near flat, and the windscreen was held onto the frame with long strips of parcel tape, the ends of which were yellowed and clinging on through arcane magick. With a K. That kind of magic(k). One door was completely missing, giving the vehicle an air of circus clown standards. Richard spat on the floor in between the skeleton's feet. "And? We don't use it, was a gift from my brother's wife, my sister. It just sits there now, so we use it to store impulse-buy packaging material in."

One of the skeletons stepped forward, took a sharp right and marched across to the car.

"Psst, hey, three-legs, what's happening?" Said the bear trap.

"Be quiet, I can barely hear them as it is."

Stopping by the car, the skeleton put his hand on the bonnet, before nodding back to his kin at the door. "We know you've been driving; it's still warm."

Richard Richardson said something in reply, his words drowned out by the bear trap.

"Go on, mate. Lift me up, let me see what's going on. All I get to see down here is the sun coming up, bit of grass waving over me, sun going down —then rinse and repeat. Do you know what kind of psychological strain that puts on you?"

Whatever was said to the main skeleton, it wasn't good. Even from his hiding position, Chaz could feel the tension rising. To his left, another group of skeletons crawled across the ground to the house, looking to sneak in through an open window. On the roof was a skeleton wearing a beret, fastening a rappel rope to the chimney, securing the end to his hip bone. Which is connected to the thigh bone.

You know the rest, sing it if you want.

"I think it's time you all got off my property before things get ugly, real ugly. If I wanna—"

"Come on, don't be a dick, be a dude. Lift me up a bit, let me see what's going on, I could offer some expert commentary and you don't even know it," the bear trap did its best to look knowledgeable and shit.

In order to try and get to the bottom of what the exchange was all about, Chaz carefully lifted the thing up so it could see the house. "Now, will you please keep quiet?"

More skeletons were encircling the house now, skittering up the walls, digging out tunnels by the side of the property and making their way underneath the shoddy foundations. The lead skeleton took a step forward, as did the rest of the ones that were lined up to attention. "You know the rules, everyone has to—"

"Whoa! Careful there, buddy, you nearly dropped me into that dog poo. Can you mind what you're doing? If I get poop on me, it's gonna be all I can taste for weeks. Honestly, some people are just so selfish, they're all me, me, me. You know what, when I came into this world—"

Chaz shook the trap. "Will you please be quiet? You wanted me to lift you up, so I did. You wanted me to let you see what was going on, so I am. But if you keep talking over them, I'm not going to know what's going on, and then I *will* let you fall into the dog muck."

"Ooh, touchy. Sounds like someone got up on the wrong side of their penis this morning. Do you ever stop to think that—"

There was a crash of glass, and Chaz looked up in time to see a group of skeletons fling themselves through the opening into the house. At the front of the building, Richard Richardson had pulled out a length of lead piping and was taking a swing at the skeleton on his porch. There was a mighty crack as it connected with the skull, but despite rocking backwards, the skeleton shook it off and jumped on top of its assailant. The rest of the skeleton crew followed suit, swamping the man, and stopping him from being able to take another wild swipe.

Screams came from within the property. Chaz dropped the bear trap which pitched forward into the pile of crap. Face down in the grass, the trap whinged. "Well, isn't this just peachy? Any chance of you righting me? Hey, pal. Pal?"

This wasn't good. Chaz had only ever seen one skeleton move before, and that was in the few seconds before the plastic model had fallen on top of him and pinned him to the doctor's floor. These things were moving about like they owned the place, and Chaz knew in that moment that he had to get the hell out of there, else he'd be the main focus of their violent attention. He slinked off further through the undergrowth, keen to use the advantage of distraction to make good his escape. He glanced across to the house as he went past, and could see other members of the Richardson family trying to fight back against the skeleton horde, to little avail. Little Roberta Richardson was mobbed as she took a wild swipe at the beret-wearing bone midget.

If this bunch of nutters couldn't deal with them, who could? Chaz knew it was very much now or never. He could see the chain link fence behind another glowing shrubbery; freedom lay beyond it —well, the Hampshire countryside, at least. He went to take a step forward when something pulled on the length of wool around his ankle. Try as he might, he couldn't move his leg. Thinking it had become snagged on a troublesome branch, or maybe even a vengeful pebble-golem, he worked his way back, stopping when he saw the problem. "What the hell are you doing? Let go!"

The bear trap had slowly chomped its way up the length of red wool, one of its eyes caked with dog bum-mud. "No," it replied through gritted teeth, "you gotta take me with you."

"I can't."

"You can and you will, or I'll keep going until I bite into that luscious leg of yours. The normal one, mind, I want to make that clear."

Chaz tried to pry the jaws open; nothing doing. "I don't need this right now."

"Then you know what you gotta do, Buster. Take me, or get bitten, I ain't choosy."

"For the love of …"

One of the skeletons that was administering some rough justice to Owen Richardson cracked its skull towards the pair, who ducked into the thicket. Man, I am loving using all these different words for *bush*. I rarely get let out into the wide open, you see, this is like a hiking holiday for me.

Waiting until the skeleton looked away, Chaz sagged. "Fine, I'll take you with me."

"Hooray! This is a great day indeed for bear traps everywhere."

"Will you let go of the wool now?"

"No chance, you'll do a runner. I'll stay gripped on for now, it doesn't seem to affect my talking at all, which is good."

Chaz stopped trying to open up the metal teeth. "What's your name? It would be good to have you referred to as something other than *bear trap*."

"Norris. Pleased to meet you, Steve."

"My name's not Steve. We've been through this in an earlier chapter, it didn't work then and it isn't going to work now. I'm Chaz, call me that. You know, my actual name."

"Someone's a bit touchy."

"Let's just get out of here, I've only been conscious for a few hours and I'm beginning to wish I'd never woken up." Picking Norris up, and allowing a bit of woollen slack, Chaz clambered over the fence at the back of the property. Landing on the other side, he counted his lucky stars –there were two of them— and headed on to Mercia Avenue, and hopefully some clues as to how to stop the skeleton menace.

Chapter
Nineteen

Chrysanthemum

After exactly a mile, Norris relented his toothy grip on Chaz's stringy link to Doggoland, and allowed the human to carry him in his arms. A few times, it tried to clamp down on some exposed skin, but with the dog crap drying to a thick crust over one eye, its depth perception was shot to shit. Pun wholly intended.

With the weight of the trap and the hassle of dragging his enormous appendage through the long grass, Chaz was relieved when he finally came upon a clearing. As the last blade of shoulder-high grass was pushed aside, he saw a group of people demolishing a small house in the middle of the field.

As he got closer, he could see that each of the four men engaged in the wanton destruction were levering varnished French baguettes off the inner walls. One of them clocked the visitor in their midst, hefted a crowbar on his shoulder, and got the attention of his bread-looting comrades. They all turned to stare at Chaz, who lumbered towards them, one hand keeping back a bitey bear trap, the other trying to hold aloft his engorged member.

"'Ere— what do you want? This is our house, we found it, so why don't you turn around and fuck off back where you came from?" The lead looter shouted, his chums joining in with some well-timed, "'ear 'ear," to emphasise that they were all countryfolk, and by implication, simpletons. Truth be told, these four were —until the whole skeleton-invasion incident— trying to excavate an underground chamber to replicate the large

110

Hadron Collider at CERN, but recent events had put paid to their earnest scientific endeavours.

Chaz pointed at the remnants of the house, which was listing badly with the support baguettes having already been half-inched. "I'm just trying to get some answers as to what the hell is happening, I don't mean any trouble."

The group had a brief conflab, eyes flickering between their illegal bread gains stuffed into carrier bags and the newcomer in their midst. After some time, which allowed Chaz to sidle closer, the self-appointed leader spoke. "We know what happened, those bloody skeletons took everything from us, we—"

"Well, not everything, just one of our arm bones," Interjector Looter interjected.

"True, but still, that led us to this path we now find ourselves on."

Angry Looter thwacked his crowbar against his nerve-dead arm. "Shut up, the pair of you. Let's just kill 'im, we'll leave his body out for the crows to feast on. Grrrrr." Because that's what angry people do, say *Grrrr* a lot.

Grrrrrr.

(Try it, though I'll warn you now, you'll get some unsavoury looks from people thinking you're angry.)

"I knew we shouldn't have come back here, we managed to get all those slices of roof tile bread yesterday, this was just pushing our luck," Despondent Looter chipped in. There, they're all labelled now, helps when it gets to the next bit, aka, the dust-up. We haven't had a good old fistfight yet, would be the perfect time to put one in before our time together is up.

"Do *you* know what's going on? What the skeletons are doing? Why everyone isn't dead or dying?" Chaz tried to appeal to them for information.

"Why the hell should we tell you anything? Eh? Grrrrrr," said the…actually, I won't insult your intelligence as I'm sure you can work out which one that was.

Despondent Looter slumped to the floor, head in hands, one of which was a bit wobbly due to having had a bone sucked out of the adjoining arm recently. "It's all gone to hell, as soon as the skeletons came into the village, we just—"

"Grrrrrr, don't tell 'im anything, you dolt. He could be one of them, a skeleton spy. Look at 'im, he's got three legs, for heaven's sake, you guys not heard of the Trojan horse? Probably got an entire platoon of elite skeletons in there, hiding in someone's body. Someone they killed and hollowed out." Interjector began to circle round Chaz, cutting off the chance of an easy escape.

Leader Looter swung his crowbar down. "E's right, you know—what's up with your leg?"

"It's a long and slightly embarrassing story, I'd rather not say."

Jabbing his crowbar towards the invader, Angry Looter spat on the floor. "Exactly what a skeleton spy would say. Grrrrrr. I've heard enough, let's smash his stupid face in." With no other warning, though I'll admit that the previous sentence is more than enough of one, he lunged at Chaz, trying to brain him with the initial blow and then pulverise his corpse until he fulfilled his aim of letting crows feast on his steaming remains.

Chaz anticipated the strike —as it was signposted a few paragraphs ago— and easily ducked to one side. As Angry's crowbar smashed into the ground, Chaz slammed Norris into the side of the man's face. The bear trap shouted with glee, "IT'S CHOMPING TIME," and crunched its jaws onto Angry's cheek. As the pair fell to the floor, the crowbar was dropped, and self-preservation kicked in as Angry tried to free himself from the trap's toothy clutches. Every pull or wrench was met with the tearing of skin as Norris ripped off strips of flesh, or yelps as the trap nipped down on fingers, taking them off at the knuckle.

"We're all going to die," Despondent wailed, before shoulder-charging Chaz and knocking him to the floor. Raising his crowbar above his head, the looter said, "I feel really bad about this, you know? But I don't really have a choice. None of us ever had a choice—"

Interrupting what would've been the final words he'd have ever heard, Chaz placed a hand under his stuffed knob and swung it upwards. The padded penis connected with Despondent, flinging him to the floor, his weapon thudding into the ground, sticking up like a looter-demise-in-waiting. Chaz rolled across to him, placed his elongated phallus over the man's face and began to suffocate the life out of him. Despondent's hands flailed as he tried to reach around the circumference of the giant pillow wang and prevent his impending murder.

Interjector stepped in. "Take this," but his personality trait was used against him, and Chaz easily ducked beneath it, whilst at the same time managing to apply more pressure to the suffocation technique he was still wholeheartedly engaged in.

The leader edged away from the fight, the senseless violence proving too much for him. He yearned for simpler times. Times he still had all his bones, and his biggest worry was hitting his digging quota each day. He looked down to see Angry sitting with his back against the front wall of the house they'd been looting —for once, not making his trademark Grrrrrr sound. Ha! He'd always been the best at the Playing Dead game, back when he was much more of a placid sort. Now he had a feral ferret trap crunching his skull open. The bone cracked and gave way before Norris tipped backwards, yelling, "BEST DAY EVER," and then diving into the brain fondue-in-waiting. The frenzied gnashing quickly turning the pink ribbed matter into lumpy slop.

To the other side, his closest pal in the entire world was enjoying the final few seconds of having air in his lungs as his attempts at ridding himself of his attacker were proving wholly futile. His hands slapped against the ground, and he fell slack. Utterly dead. UTTERLY, I TELL YOU.

All the while, Interjector was trying to smack the man in their midst who probably didn't want to steal their bread after all. Every mad swing was easily avoided, tiring him a little more with every lazy swipe. The leader wanted to run but was transfixed by the grisly sight playing out in front of him. He walked into a tree trunk and slid down its length, sitting cross-legged on the floor.

"Gimme…a…minute, will ya?" Interjector was doubled over, the exertion of three dozen swings and misses having completely shagged him out.

Fresh from killing one man, Chaz stood up, tossing his killer appendage from one hand to the other. "I'll give you a chance to live. Turn around and go. Now. If you don't, you'll end up like—"

"Fair enough, you don't have to tell me twice," Interjector said, picking out a random spot in the distance and setting course for it, burning with adrenalin. Unfortunately, he didn't see the bright red woollen string, tripped over it and pitched straight onto Despondent's crowbar, you remember? The one I mentioned a little way back and made a big deal out of it. That one.

There were two audible gasps from the surviving humans as they heard the shucking sound of the crowbar piercing the chest, spearing the heart, and bursting through the man's back, holding the pilfered organ aloft as if it had been dropped and a good Samaritan was holding it out for its owner to reclaim.

The only sound now was that of Norris swimming around inside the rapidly diminishing skull pan he was in. Having liquified the brain, it was trying to mulch as much of the head innards as possible. The leader rested against the tall stalk behind him, wondering why it was warm to the touch and pulsing against his skin like an early morning boner pressed into his back.

It wasn't a wholly unpleasant sensation, but it was one that fired up the keen investigative mind he had once used on a daily basis before melancholy gave way to the looting of varnished baked goods. Leader slowly turned around to face the thick stem. He ran his hands over the surface, gulping as it undulated with the movement. He could feel something press against his hands from the other side, as if a mirror version of him was trying to cop a feel. He pressed an ear against the stalk and could hear liquid sloshing around within.

A sound like the crotch on a pair of trousers splitting – don't pretend you don't know what that sounds like, we *all* do— jolted him backwards. A slit had opened up, and green sap trickled from the opening. As the tear ran further down the stem, it began to widen. From the sticky mulch, Leader could see a pair of bulging eyes; no eyelids held them in place, so they gawked back completely unhindered by skin.

"What the?..." was all Leader could muster, as the staring eyes were a mere diversion. His body rocked as something from within the stalk burst free and slammed into the bottom of his ribcage. Leader looked down to see two near-skeletal arms forming a bridge from the sticky sap innards to his guts. He laughed involuntarily as he felt something tickle his liver, only then realising that whatever was inside the stem was now inside him.

Bony fingers rifled through his digestive tract, swishing and swiping with wilful abandon. One minute he thought he needed a huge poo, as his colon was gripped like someone testing the ripeness of a melon; the next, a big piss, as his bladder was squeezed and kneaded. As the festival of odd sensations set up camp within his torso, he experienced an altogether new sensation, feeling something wet and slippery tumble from the hole that had been made in his stomach. Leader looked down to see that one hand was still rooting around inside him. The other had withdrawn from the hidden sanctuary, but the metal watch strap —pinning a glove of skin to the wrist— had become snagged on his large intestine.

The more thrashing from both parties that went on, the more intestine would get tugged from the incision. It was getting to the stage where it looped down, swinging against Leader's knees, the denim turning red, the coarse fabric making the once-slick gut rope dry and leathery.

Sensing that all was not going according to plan, the other hand quit its part-time job of flicking internal organs and retracted to help its sibling free itself from the coiling pile of steaming evacuation-tubing, which was piling up on the floor. After a few seconds, and little success, a head with its skin almost dissolved pushed itself free from its plant-tomb. "Gith me a minuth," it lisped, annoyed with itsthelf (sorry —its*elf)* as much as anything. Leader gave a weak thumbs up, trying to focus on the scene in front of him and ignoring the nagging thought that he'd have to somehow scoop all this stuff back inside at some point.

The body invader managed to pry a fingernail underneath the catch of the wristwatch, and tried to lift it up, doing little except peel the nail easily off the bone, as if it were a sticker on a banana. "For fuckth sakth." With the thumb now shorn of skin and nail, the end of the bone easily dug under the clip and pulled it free. The watch, now decoupled from itself, rotated to one side before hitting the floor. "Da dah," the sticky head shouted, just as the rest of Leader's guts plopped out of the freshly-formed cavity onto the floor, quickly followed by its owner, who lay on top of his own intestines like a workshy layabout.

"Oopsy," the head mumbled. Eager to give the man a bit of a kick and see if that would help with the revival process, the figure placed its hands either side of the vulvic opening and pulled. As it was delivered into the world, there was a surprising development.

"What the?..." Chaz mumbled, looking across at the plant —and whatever was coming out of it. Like twins, just behind the birth of head number one, was another. This was as rancid as the first, though smaller. As a broad pair of shoulders heaved out of the slit, the mouth on the bigger head gurned as if it were chewing on a ball of gristle. With the shoulders free, Chaz saw another pair of arms slip out of the confines of the plant, these were smaller than the pair that were pushing themselves free. Seeing Chaz standing watching events unfurl but doing little to help, the big head asked, "Whath year ith it?" Getting nothing in reply, it growled, "Are youth going thoo help?"

"Okay ..." Chaz offered his hands reluctantly, dreading what the gunk would feel like against his skin. He was right to be worried, as four bony hands closed around his own It reminded him of the time his brother had thrown up into his hands and then slipped on a loose paving slab, instinctively reaching out and grabbing hold of Chaz's arms, dragging them both onto the puke-stained floor.

Stifling his own upchuck, Chaz looked away, dug his heels in and heaved backwards. With the worst bit of the heads and shoulders already breached, and the bodies slick with floral gunk and rotting body juices, the remainder of the body slipped free from the green womb and was delivered upon the floor.

Chaz let go and wiped the crap off his skin using the Leader's shirt as a towel. In front of him, the twin heads looked up at the sky, the body squirming and writhing against the itchy ground, reacting to their caesarean birth. After a few minutes —and realising that no midwife was going to come and smack their backsides and swaddle them in a comfy towel— the *thing* realised that if it was going to get up, it would have to do so under its own steam, as Chaz was really not keen on lending another hand, having just cleaned off the slime from the first go.

Scrabbling to its feet, of which it seemed to have more than necessary, the newborn creature panted with exertion. The big head lolled to the ground, trying to catch its breath. It stood in a growing puddle of blood and half-digested food, spreading out from the ruin of Leader's ripped intestinal tract. It caught its reflection in the puddle, fingers running over its body and construction. Faded memories kicked back in, but what looked back did not match. The two heads sat atop one grotesque body; two ribcages fused together. From each side sprung two arms, the top ones large, the bottom set smaller. This was repeated with its legs: two larger limbs supported its distended form, with two smaller ones —parodies of the other— hanging down the side like evolutionary droppings. Perhaps they were just decoration? They flicked out, trying to gain purchase on the ground, but failing.

"Waith a momenth." The mass of limbs bent over and picked up its wristwatch. With the timepiece back where it belonged, it turned slowly towards Chaz, who was trying to pick pieces of melted skin from underneath his fingernails. The three heads all looked at each other. "Thith ith just…" the main head flicked forwards, expelling a fountain of bright yellow vomit over their involuntary midwife. This continued for some time. Way longer than it should, to be honest. After some dry heaving, fingers reached inside what remained of the throat and pulled out lengths of stringy veins.

With the smaller hands patting their collective back, they felt freer. "That's better." A hand smacked over the mouth in shock before remembering that the voice was its own. Wanting to test it out some more, it decided to say its favourite thing. "You're a complete and total fucknut."

Well, this was something. Huh? You didn't see this coming, eh?

You did? Of *course* you did. Like you saw him get eaten by that big fuck off flower?

Whatever.

Sensing that he was alive again, in some form at least, Harry turned to the left and looked at the smaller head. "And who the fuck do you think you are?"

"Me," came the shy response.

"Oh, great. It's the greatest witch that ever there was. Not."

Chaz coughed a pissed off and attention-seeking cough; you know the one, where you're pissed off and want some attention. It was hard to ignore him, standing as he was, covered in luminescent vomit. "Excuse me?"

"No need to apologise, mate."

"I think you're the one that owes me an apology and an explanation."

The ex-detective sidled up to the man. "I'm Harry Surge, and that prick Barnaby went and took me out, but not before showing me what he'd been doing with all those bones he'd been nicking out of people."

"The skeleton army?"

"Thems the wankers. I was hot on the trail —before he offed me, that is."

"You weren't," Sally offered.

"Shut up. I'm the one telling the story. Anyway, who the dick are you?"

"I'm Chaz. I've been in a coma the entire time, woke up a few hours ago and this …"

Harry pretended to cry. "Boo-fucking-hoo, princess. Look at me. I should be dead, *we* should be dead, instead we've been slowly eaten away for…however long it's been. You don't see me crying about it, do you?"

"Well, no, but—"

"And look at me. Fucking hell, I've got the woman melded to me that let the bastard grow all those flowers in the first place. Shit, least you've still got all your bones, by the looks of it." Harry looked down at the man's lower half. "And three legs. Is that a new thing?"

Chaz was scraping the sick from his face, scratching so hard that his cheeks were turning red. "Well, erm…"

Harry clicked his fingers. "I know you. You're the one who had the tiny dick. The one from the hospital. You know, the one whose bird was the first victim." Harry leant forwards and patted Chaz's penis. "Man, that must feel odd. Of course, when you're as well-endowed as me…" He said, standing proud, hands on hips.

"Yeah?"

"Well, I know *I* won't need to worry about getting my schlong longered."

Chaz began to laugh, still mopping himself down. "Right…cos yours is so big."

"Uh-huh, that's right."

"Have you seen it recently?"

"Well, no, but why would I—" Harry looked down to see something akin to the last hot dog on the butcher's display, albeit a hot dog with its skin torn open and gobbets of mechanically-removed meat dribbling from the hole. "Motherfucker."

One of the small arms rose up and pointed at the dismantled shack. "Gone."

"Who gives a shit about your crappy house? Look at my knob. El Capitan looks like he's been chewed on by a pack of rabid wolves. The things he's been in, the things he's seen."

Chaz wrung out the Leader's shirt, which was now drenched in vomit. "This is all very interesting and all, but it's not really helping. I'm trying to get to the bottom of how these skeletons came about in the first place, and you come along to add another layer of mystery. As I said, I've been—"

"Yes, in a fucking coma. We get it. Everyone gets it. You've had an exceptionally difficult life and now it's just got even harder. BIG FUCKING DEAL. We were eaten by a plant, and I'm now sharing what passes for a nervous system with Mustang Sally here. I don't care how I'm back, the important thing is that I am. Let's not delve too deeply into the details, okay? Look, how about we make a deal?"

"What do you propose?"

"Me and the dumbest witch in Hampshire can give you the lowdown on how this all happened if you take us back to your pad so we can work out a plan of attack. Coz right now, the only thing I want to do is find the fat bastard who turned me into a really crappy Goro."

Sally tapped their shared shoulder. "Who?"

"Are you shitting me? Come on, you're gonna have to get with the times. Look, that's not important right now —are you both in or out?"

"Out," Sally answered quickly.

Harry's rancid head laughed. "Doesn't really matter, my legs are the only ones touching the ground, so I'm the one calling the shots, sister. What about you, King Soft Knob?"

"I guess I'm in, but can you lay off the swearing a bit, please?"

"Of course I can, you cunting arseface. Now, what's the quickest way back to your gaff? You got a car round here or something?"

Chaz dropped the sodden shirt to the ground, knelt down and wrapped a finger round the red wool. "Not exactly, I think you best grab hold of me. We're …outta twine," he chuckled.

Harry grabbed hold of the man and sighed. "That supposed to be a Back to the Future pun?"

"Yeah."

"Bit shit, wasn't it?"

"I thought it was good."

"Hey guys. Don't forget about me!" A voice echoed within a bone chamber.

The detective looked across to the source of the words. "Okay…there appears to be a shit-covered, engorged, tiny bear trap wallowing inside that man's skull. Is he with you?"

"Kinda. Can one of you…both of you…grab him, please?"

Sally answered. "Sure."

"Just be careful, he's a bit bitey."

With Norris tucked under an armpit, his desire to eat diminished by the putrid flesh that was pressed against his steel teeth, Harry and Sally clung onto Chaz. "Right, hold on tight," he said, before he pulled on the string seventeen times.

Chapter
Twenty

Primula vulgaris

From the additional effort it was taking to reel in his new BFF, Venkatesh could tell something was amiss. Of all the possibilities running through his mind, the one he settled on was that Chaz's penis had dipped into an expanse of water and become waterlogged, thus explaining the weight differential. It came as a shock when the truth was being reeled in across the rubbish-strewn car park.

"Come on girls, get ready for Daddy Singh," he shouted to his dogs, some of whom responded by growling and baring their teeth while the others indulged in a post-milking session snooze. As Chaz and his new guest got closer, Venkatesh began to panic. Was this one of the skeletons he'd heard so much about? If it was, then this one must've been a reject, as it appeared to be two fused together, and still in possession of some of their flesh and hard-to-remove bits and bobs.

Still, he pulled them in, figuring it would be easier to dispatch the newcomer inside than venturing outdoors and run the risk of encountering other people. With the guest sat on Chaz's lap, riding him like a sled, his lidless eyes met Singh's and a flash of recognition sparked in them, quickly followed by the abomination, mouthing, "Oh for the love of god, not *him*."

Chaz went to stand up, forcing the lap-rider to disembark. Singh ushered them all inside, into a braying semi-circle of dogs. No sooner had the front doors been slammed shut than some of the canines lost interest, sensing that one of the newbies had been before, and the other one smelled decidedly rank. A curious Jack Russell went to sniff the decrepit person's bum but was shooed away with a rolled-up newspaper, which Harry had unwittingly collected on his sojourn across the concrete tundra.

After wrapping chains around the handles, Singh fell back against the doors, eyeing up the new arrival. He turned to his new chum. "Are you okay?"

"Fine, thanks, it's pretty weird out there. The skeletons are tiny. You wouldn't think they'd be much of a threat, but they pacified the Richardsons in no time at all."

"Cool. Beans. Cool beans. Who's your new *pal*? Did you find them in the Richardsons' crap heap out back?"

"No, I—"

"Doctor Singh, don't you recognise me?" Harry interrupted.

"No, I don't recall sneezing you out." He looked around for someone to high-five but found no willing participants. Seeking solace in the fact that *he* thought he was hilarious —a trait I share with my fictional character— Singh surveyed the thing that stood in front of him. "Your voice sounds a little familiar, but I can't quite place the face."

"You think you're a fucking comedian, you milk-sniffing dickhead?"

"Sometimes. And how do you know about my hobby?"

Harry took a step forward and patted the ex-doctor's bulging paunch, leaving a pale green handprint on the fabric. "Still not worked all those biscuits off, have you?"

Venkatesh gasped; the kind of gasp that only comes with a shocking and sudden revelation. "Detective?"

"The one and the same, looks like you're finally fulfilling your deepest desires," Harry said, waving an arm at the dogs, all of whom had given up the pretence of being guard dogs and who were engaged in the more standard canine behaviours.

"Who's your friend?" Singh asked, whilst doing a lap around the detective.

"This here is Sally, the witch who helped Barnaby grow all the flowers which have led to the downfall of Hampshire society, at least, maybe even the world."

Singh balled his fists. "She did *what*?"

"Not me," she muttered, her head looking around the derelict hospital, wondering how big the baguettes must be to support such a structure.

"You cost me everything."

"Nice dogs," Sally replied.

"Well…yes…they are, but that's not the point. I'd still be a doctor helping people if it wasn't for you."

Harry moved his head forward, closer to the man. "You can punch her if you want."

"Eh?"

"A quick jab. I won't judge you, just don't swing and miss and mash my one remaining ear, that would proper fuck me off."

Chaz stood between the two, hands outstretched. "Come on, now, things might have taken a diversion from normality into the maybe-apocalypse, but this really isn't on. No one is punching anyone, okay?"

"I might punch you if you continue speaking," Harry warned.

Venkatesh backed away. "You're right, I'm a lover, not a fighter. I'm sorry. It's just…all this is so much to take in, you know? Up until a few hours ago, I hadn't spoken to another conscious person for three weeks. Only you as you slept…I like doing that. And now? You came into my life, then you left, then you came back again —and with the man I thought would stop all the madness before it started. But he didn't. And the woman who helped start it is melted onto his body, and despite my low-calorie diet I still haven't shifted the extra weight. Just been quite an emotional day, that's all."

Chaz consoled the doctor, who sobbed gently into the embrace. Harry tapped the three-legged man on the shoulder. "Why is he being such a wuss? Like, MAN THE FUCK UP ALREADY."

"Shh, there's nothing wrong with showing your feelings, you know. Tough love never worked."

"Pfft, whatever, Big Knob Cheese, my mum did the whole tough love thing on me and I turned out fine." Harry rested his hands on what remained of his hips. Part of the mulch that was his right bum cheek separated from the bone and dripped onto the floor, hitting the lino with a wet SPLAT.

"Yeah," Chaz mumbled, "you've turned out perfectly."

"I know sarcasm when I hear it, and my radar just went BING-A-FUCKING-BONG."

"Look, I don't want to get into this n-OWWWWWWW," Chaz leapt off the ground, ruining the moment.

Harry adopted his best Queensbury rules-style boxing stance. "Is it one of the skeletons? It is, isn't it? Has one burrowed its way into you through the old one-eyed trouser-python and sliced open your guts to launch a surprise raid?"

"NO!" Chaz screamed and turned around, revealing Norris well and truly clamped onto his shoulder.

The bear trap rolled its one good eye around the people who were gawping at it. "What? It's what I do, I CHOMP on things. Leave me unattended for too long and CHOMP, that's it, I'm off again. Man, your skin is really nice and tender, can I bite your face off?"

"No, I'm using it!"

"What the hell is that?"

Norris leaned to one side so he could get a good look at Singh. "What do you think I am? I'm a frigging bear trap. Mmmm, your throat looks really yummy, would you mind if I nibbled on it a bit?"

"No way."

"Go on, just a little bit, I won't drink *all* your blood."

"Not a chance."

"How about I just pull out a length of your artery, help pick out the bits of brain from earlier?"

"What brains? Earlier? Why…why are you talking to me? Chaz?"

Harry grabbed hold of the bear trap, nodded to Sally to put her little legs on the man's back, and whispered in Chaz's ear. "This may sting a bit." With an abrupt tug and Sally's expert foot anchoring, Harry managed to remove the trap with only a small section of skin being ripped off. Chaz screamed and clamped a hand on his back, trying (and failing) to staunch the blood loss.

"Nom nom nom, aww, why did you take me off? I was enjoying that."

Pulling Chaz in close, Singh peeled away the man's fingers and examined the wound. "It's not too deep, come on, I can deal with it." Harry rested the snapping Norris on top of a bin, making sure he didn't get to close to it.

"Argh, my shoulder! My head! Argh!" Chaz screamed, clutching each body part in turn, thinking that would be the best way forward when it came to pain management. His skin was flushed and covered in beads of sweat. He lamented his aches and pains once more, before collapsing onto the floor, his leg kicking out as if it were trying to remove an errant hedgehog.

"What's eating him?" Norris asked. "And why isn't it me?"

Venkatesh scooped Chaz up by putting his sweaty arm around his shoulder. "I'm going to see if I can find out what's wrong with him. You two stay here, and don't go near my vintage milk." He pointed at Harry, who was too busy trying to affix his missing bum cheek back in its rightful place. As Singh carried Chaz down to the annexe that had borne witness to his own catastrophe, he called over his shoulder, "When I get back, I want some answers. None of you are making any sense today."

(How bloody charming! Here I am, trying to make this as entertaining and memorable as possible, and the characters that I MADE WITH MY OWN BRAIN are giving me hassle. I don't know why I bother sometimes. I'm going to sack this off and have some me-time.)

Chapter Twenty One

Fritillaria meleagris

Harry was bored. Not just that, but Sally had fallen asleep a few hours back and had been snoring into his ear for most of that time. He'd tried to stir her in a number of ways, starting with a gentle rousing, through cheek slapping (or what remained of them; jawbone slapping would be more appropriate) and all the way up to sticking a finger through her nose cavity to try and poke the decaying remains of her brain.

Nothing had worked. The plastic seat was uncomfortable too; he sat lopsided after failing to reattach his buttock. Now, he squidged the gelatinous mass between his bony fingers, thinking of ways in which he could murder the snoring witch without messing himself up even more in the process. He didn't really fancy lugging around her dead body until the end of time itself, so had been trying to source surgical tools to lop off her limbs and head.

So far, he'd managed to retrieve Singh's scalpel —which was as blunt as Harry's demeanour— and a length of dental floss. As he was testing the slicing ability of the latter, Singh stumbled through the double doors back into the waiting room. His appearance did little to assuage the assumption that things had gone really well in the 'making Chaz better' stakes, as he was covered head to toe in blood and tufts of padding. Aside from a brief return to the room to pick up the snappy bear trap just after hour two began, neither man nor trap had been seen since. "What's up, Doc?" Harry wished right there and then that he had a carrot, even though he was sure he could no longer eat food of any description.

The poor man looked distracted; I guess numerous hours in a powered-down building, performing surgery on the person who had rekindled your social life could be a good explanation for that. He slumped down in the chair opposite the Harry/Sally mutant and let out an enormous sigh. "It's all over."

Harry tried to remember his training about dealing with bad news and people, but could only recall an old episode of Mork and Mindy. "Damn, I barely knew him, but he didn't deserve to die. Not like that. Not now."

Singh let out a hysterical chuckle. "Oh no. He's not dead. Just …"

"What, Doc? What happened?"

"The bite…between the rusting metal jaws of Norris and the bacteria in the dog poop…Chaz got infected. It was bad. Real bad."

"Is he going to be okay?"

"I guess, I mean…he's still alive. Of a fashion."

"What do you mean, 'of a fashion'? Have you turned him into a pair of casual slacks? Do people still use the word *slacks* anymore?"

Venkatesh met the detective's searching gaze. "In time…he may wish that was the case. He's …"

"What?"

"He's …"

"WHAT?"

"He's …"

Harry stood up, jolting Sally awake for a few seconds before she nodded off again. Harry slapped Singh across the face. "That's for starters, now will you tell me what the fuck has happened, or I'm going to tie your arms together and tickle your feet."

Nursing his face, Singh stood up and gestured towards the darkened annexe. "Why don't you see for yourself…Detective. Chaz…please, come in. We're expecting you."

A leaden silence befell the vast room; even Sally knew that something big was brewing in this little shindig of a story, and stopped burbling in her sleep for the next bit. Dogs that had been chowing down noisily on their dinner, stopped. All eyes turned to the dingy room; the once proud electronic doors half-open. From within came a shuffling sound as feet struggled to lift off, instead skating across the grimy lino. Singh sunk into the chair, his hands over his mouth, trying to hold in the nervous laughter, knowing what the others would see any moment now. How they would soon look upon the true face of madness. Of desperation. Of the result of hastily scavenged medical supplies and knowledge.

"Guys?" A surprisingly human voice asked from the gloom. One of the doors buckled as something clattered into it.

Fingers wrapped around the edge of the door and Harry let out the air he'd been saving for a rainy day. "Phew, he's still a man, at least. I was worried you'd scooped his brain out and sellotaped it to one of your dogs."

Venkatesh scraped his fingernails down his own temple and cheeks. "If only that were an option. Chaz was too far gone for that. The infection…it moved fast, it was in his blood, you see. His own life force became his greatest enemy. By the time I'd got him on the operating table, his brain was ruined, turned to mulch by the insidious invader. I had to think fast, and after I managed to stabilise his body, I had a tough choice to make."

"Guys? I can hear you…I think. I don't feel right…I feel funny, what's happened to me?" Chaz's enormous member pushed the door open. The bottom half of his body was naked, and if it wasn't for the hair, it would be impossible to know which bit was which. His torso and head were still swathed in night.

"What did you do, Singh? WHAT DID YOU DO?"

"I did the only thing I could. I took an oath to save people no matter how far gone they were, at any cost."

"How did you save him? Tell me."

As Chaz stumbled from the doorway into the light, Singh rushed to be by his side, making sure he didn't snag anything on the door's pointy bits. As the morning sun streaked through the windows, it illuminated the patient's body from the bottom up. Harry shrieked, jerking Sally awake. She rubbed her sleepy eyes, looked at the man opposite, and added her own shriek to the alarm. Chaz stopped, his hands patting his body, sensing that something had changed (again), but he was unsure what. His hands felt ragged tufts of skin around his neck, before settling on something where his head should be. "My god, his head, it's—" Harry blurted out.

"It's a trap!" Singh shouted, both ruining the big reveal I'd been leading up to and mocking me by cackling in the exact way you'd expect a mad professor to do. Make that noise right now —out loud if you're brave enough, or in your head, if you're not. It was that *exact* sound.

Harry kicked Venkatesh in the bollocks, making the doctor shut up and sink to the ground as if he had just been kicked in the bollocks. Because he had. Harry loomed over the stricken man. "No you fucking don't. No more pop-culture references in this one, not after hungry nuns. I let the whole Back to the Future *outta twine* thing slide a while back, but I'm not having any more of that nonsense."

Struggling to get the words out through gritted teeth, Singh managed. "What was wrong with that book? I thought it was quite funny."

"We all did. Hell, I had chums who had *that* flashback scene stuck in their heads for weeks. But some …well, they thought it got tiresome, that the writer was relying on other's work instead of making up their own nonsense. So, no. You so much as make one more pop-culture reference, I'm going to saw your nipples off and screw them to your eyeballs," Harry said, waving a balled fist at the doctor, who was still massaging his swollen pant-plums.

Chaz coughed loudly. "Excuse me, I don't really want loads of sympathy, but I've undergone a life-changing event here and it would be nice to get some support."

"Well, it's two now, isn't it?" Harry added.

"Two?"

Sidling up to the man with a shrunken bear trap for a head and noticing the expert stapling that was keeping the metal trap firmly ensconced in the neck, Harry patted Chaz's dick-leg. "You forgotten about this already? Or hoping that the new addition would detract from it?"

"Course not, just this one feels a bit more of a substantial change, you know? Just when I thought my luck was changing…"

Harry ducked behind Chaz, and turned back to Venkatesh. "Where's his human head?"

Still clutching his man-eggs, but standing at least, Venkatesh managed a pained reply. "What do you mean?"

"Well, I thought you would've stuck it to his backside, or shrunk it down and mounted it on one of his shoulders. I'm a bit disappointed, if I'm being honest."

"That's a point, where *is* my head?"

Singh managed to sit down, the pain easing slightly. "I told you, it was too far gone, too infected. It became clear early on that the only way I could save you was to introduce something to your body that would be able to deal with the infection, and…well, since the bear trap—"

"My name is Norris," the trap intoned, a little stunned he'd said anything.

"Anyway…since *Norris* was the incubator of the malaise, I figured that he must be able to deal with the symptoms, so I made a difficult decision."

"Of chopping my head off and replacing it with a poo-smeared, talking bear trap?" Chaz uttered, his tone bordering on combative.

"I swore to myself, after everything that happened, that I would never treat another living person. But I couldn't let you die. And if I'd done nothing, that's exactly what would've happened."

Another heavy silence hung in the air, before Harry helpfully added, "Well, this is fucking weak, isn't it? I've died and come back as two people, and now giant club-dick has got his own little fucking addition too. You already have the penis thing going on, why did you have to try and muscle in on my unique twist?"

"I didn't choose to have a bear trap for a head."

"Norris, my name is Norris," the bear trap shouted afterwards. Which was getting strange as they're both coming from the same mouth and in the same voice. I need to nip this in the bud, fast.

Singh rooted around in his doctor's white coat, and after finding (and discarding) a set square, four D20, a Theremin called Gerald and a freshly exclaimed exclamation mark, he held aloft a screwdriver. "Tip your head forward a minute, I'll sort this out."

With Chaz doing as he was told, Venkatesh lifted up a flap of skin which he'd made purposefully at the join between trap and skin, and put the screwdriver head into the groove of a screw. Which is what you do with screwdrivers, just so you know. There were three settings, C, N and C/N. I'm sure you can work out which ones mean which. With it currently in the C/N setting, he switched it to N, just to emphasise the point. "Go on, Chaz, say something."

"It's Norris, you fool. Now give me something to chomp, NOM NOM NOM."

Twisting the screwdriver up to C, Singh repeated,

"Go on, Chaz, say something."

"Can someone pass me a flannel, please, there's something smeared on my phallus."

Singh replaced the flap of skin and folded his arms. "There you go, Detective, happy now?"

"Fucking elated. Though we've spent more than enough time back here, more than I'd wanted to. Let's get on with it."

"What's the plan now?" Singh asked.

"The same as it was before, find Barnaby and fuck him right up. I'm going to sneak into town and try to find out what the score is, we're going to need some wheels, though."

Chaz clapped his hands together. "Excellent, let's get going."

"Oh no you don't," Harry said, pressing a sticky hand against Chaz's chest. "This next bit was done before you were written back into this little story, so I'm going all lone wolf. You stay here with the doctor —who also shouldn't be in this part of the book— and chill out. Milk some dogs, have a shit, whatever, just try not to let the wacko carry out any more improvements on you, okay?"

Sally's head tipped forward, making one of those really loud snore/snort things that always wakes you up, especially if you're on a train or in a meeting at work. "And me."

"Yeah…and you. Come on, Sleepy Sally, let's go find out what the hell is going on. We've got shitloads of wrongs to right, the main one being killing me. Because I'm so fucking great. Let's get this parade of arse-kicking into action."

"Hang on." Singh rummaged around in his pockets once more, eventually pulling out a plastic kazoo, thrusting it into the detective's hand. "Here, take this. If you need to summon us, toot three times and we'll be there."

"Thanks, although …if you *are* needed, then it's going to involve even more rewrites. I just hope this shit still makes sense afterwards, or people are going to give it really shite reviews."

(To be honest, I think you should. Just to spite me.)

Chapter
Twenty
Two

Symphyotrichum oblongifolium

Luckily for the disgusting melded-together duo, all the waiting around in the hospital had meant that they didn't venture out until the early hours of the morning. This had the added bonus that the only things (other than them) stalking the village cul-de-sacs were cats or part-time politicians looking to cash in on the latest environmental disaster. Curious to find out what exactly was going on, they stole a newspaper that had been wedged into an obstinate letterbox.

Expecting/hoping for a blood-soaked civil war and some z-list celebrity pimping their latest venture capital scheme, Harry was pissed off that the headline, 'YOGURT TOUCHED MY KNEE INAPPROPRIATELY' was exceedingly mundane.

When he was being slowly digested within the inner workings of the orchid, the only thing that kept him going was that it if he did ever escape, it would at least be the end of days. You know the kind. Loads of dead bodies being picked on by carrion. Blown-out windows, looters, vigilante groups stringing people up on lampposts for having the temerity to steal the last Weetabix from their supplies. Roving bands of marauders in stripped-down and tooled-up cars prowling the rubbish strewn highways, looking for people to run over —and some phonetic switcheroo of petrol. "We need guzzoline/gazz/petaroll," insert whichever word you want into that little sentence, which is actually you speaking, by the way. You ascended the ranks of that group of bandits pretty quickly. Well done.

But instead, it was just like every other Wednesday he'd had. A complete and total fucking let-down. Some call it hump day, but let's be honest, it's a nothing day. Far enough away from the last weekend, but not close enough to the next. Harry had spent most Wednesdays knocking up homemade 'Wanted' posters, catching up on the tedium of policework. This Wednesday, though, he'd break the habit of a lifetime and get out there.

Well, he kinda had to. If anyone saw him in his current state, it was likely that they would batter him with the closest thing to hand or find a humungous Kleenex to try and wrap him up in before disposing of the lot in the nearest bin.

First things first. The witch was evidently still annoyed with being second-in-command of the whole legs-in-charge deal, as every step he'd taken since leaving the hospital had been accompanied by her kicking him in the back of his thighs. "Knock it off, will ya? I'll let you have a go later when I'm pissed, deal?" This stopped her for a little bit, but only until he came up with the next step of his plan. "We need to get our hands on a car, ideally with some small degree of violence —but not too much. Then we need to find out what the fuck that bony bastard Barnaby is up to. This place is way too quiet, there should be some death and destruction somewhere, we just gotta find it. Unless ..." Harry tried to peek into the closest house, checking for signs of life. "Perhaps everyone is dead? His horde of skeletons have killed all humans and those bastards we met in the field were the last ones left alive? If so, that means we've extinguished the flickering candle of humanity, and I'm surprisingly chipper about it."

"No," Sally pointed towards a kitchen window opposite where a woman was busy strangling a swan.

"Classy. We need to work out how we can get into that house, render her unconscious, nick her keys and borrow her car, okay?"

"No."

"Don't get all high and mighty. I figured you'd be against it, so just be a silent conscientious objector for the next five minutes, okay?"

"Fine."

Harry slapped her cheek gently. As his hand came back it did so with strings of bloody mucus. "Good on ya. Now, no screaming, no noise, we do this real quiet like…"

With everything that had been going on the last three weeks, Denise Upton-Smyth had been on edge. She was having issues at work *before* losing an arm bone, and when you're a professional arm wrestler, that shit impacts you more than most. Granted, most of her local competitors had, too, but with the rest of the country lagging behind and being infected last, she'd seen her rankings slide.

The only thing that helped her to get through the day and her slowly crumbling hopes and dreams was her burgeoning reliance on murdering and devouring the local avian wildlife.

It had started off unintentionally. Whilst attempting to fetch milk from the fridge to pour onto her morning Proteinator Flakes, she accidentally shut a passing pigeon in the door, breaking its neck. At first, she was aghast, then with some seasoning and the right application of heat, discovered that the combination of bird and breakfast cereal was a culinary delight.

From there, it escalated slowly; hard-boiled eggs were hollowed out and replaced with steamed baby duckling, Denise using toast soldiers to dip into the succulent meat. The humble Blue Tit was added to her lunchtime minestrone soup. Before long, all her meals were being levelled up with winged creatures.

This fateful morning, having woken up on the sofa still spooning the swan she had lured back to her house the previous night with the promise of golden things, she realised it was getting out of hand. Deciding to end her killing spree with the most taboo of birds, she finally managed to put the poor thing out of its misery just as she heard the kitchen door handle squeak. As the wooden door rattled in its frame, Denise staggered over to it, and pulled it open. "Yes? Can I help you?"

Having been rumbled, the Harry/Sally monstrosity stood up to full height, their skin glistening in the early morning sun as fresh pus weeped from unsealed joins between bone and rotting flesh. "Erm …" Harry mumbled.

"Yeah. What?"

"We're here to read your meter?"

"Bit keen, aren't you?"

"Yeah, we're…erm…on a special bonus scheme. Any we get before nine o'clock gives us double."

Denise eyed them up. Something about them didn't add up. Two heads. Two bodies —sort of, they were fused together, but still. Four arms. Four legs. "Are you sure you're from the electric company?"

"Erm, yes. Of course we are."

"Why do you have all these extra…bits?"

Harry clicked his fingers. "All the electricity on your street comes from nuclear power you see, they wanted to promote people from within; in our case, from within the highly radioactive core."

The woman looked the monstrosity up and down. "Hmmm."

"Can we read your meter *please*? Go on, help us out. It's a hard life out in the real world for us, competing against people with the correct number of heads and still in possession of their own skin."

Denise caved, eager to shove a garlic bulb up the swan's arsehole and get roasting it. "Fine, I'll just open the back gate," she said, turning her back on the oddity and heading back inside the kitchen.

Harry stepped inside, picked up the bone-hard carcass of a cured goose and twonked the woman on the back of the head. "KABOSHAROO!" Denise faceplanted the floor and did a brief horizontal Riverdance before adopting the more orthodox approach of remaining motionless.

"Why?" Sally whispered.

"She may have bought it to begin with, but there's no telling how long our cover story would've lasted. Best to incapacitate her now than struggle with her when she works out we're not on the level."

Sally pointed to the prone woman. "Dead."

"No she fucking isn't, I only tapped her, look." Harry nudged the woman's leg with his toes. Denise's body shifted forwards and a puddle of lumpy blood began to bloom outwards from her smashed-in brain container.

"See."

"I didn't mean to, just wanted to knock her out, not make a skull flap straight into Hypothalamus Central. Jesus, I thought it was bad enough looking at your ugly mug, but that is something else entirely." Harry picked up a dirty tea towel and draped it over the back of Denise's caved-in head. "Better, now let's get the keys and get the fuck out of here. Still, one good thing."

"What?"

Harry held his hands up. "No fingerprints, good luck pinning this on me." He crouched down by the body, which was twitching a little —as bodies tend to do in this sort of situation. It's pretty off-putting, but you get used to it. He shoved a hand into her pocket and began to root around, pulling out a ten-pound note and a Dictaphone which played a medley of alluring bird song. "Score!"

He checked the other pocket and finally managed to retrieve a set of keys. Standing up, Harry began to laugh.

"What?"

Jiggling on the spot, Sally's limbs began to flail about wildly. "Let's bounce. You get it? Coz you're bouncing up and down like a sheep on a bungie cord."

"Great."

"You're a right barrel of laughs, aren't ya? Fucking hell. After I sort all this out, and saved the world, I'm gonna see if some hot doctor —definitely not the weirdo at the end of this kazoo— can cut you off me. You're proper cramping my style."

Chapter
Twenty
Three

Hydrangea macrophylla

Denise's car turned out to be the shell of a Ford Fiesta draped over a ride-on lawnmower. Evidently with her decrease in earnings, she'd been forced to make some sacrifices, and her automobile was one of them. So, in the wee hours of the morning, with his body count since his second coming standing at two, Harry and his conjoined pal were buzzing through the back streets of Charlton, girding their mulched loins for trouble.

"They could be anywhere, try and look behind us if you can. Be the rear-view mirror, since this fucking liability doesn't have one," Harry said, revving up the crappy motor and chugging on down the road.

They'd only been going five minutes and still hadn't left the estate; in that time they hadn't seen anyone in the flesh, but closed curtains, the sound of televisions blaring and that general lived-in vibe put the shits up Harry more than anything.

"I just don't get it. Why raise a skeleton army if you're not going to murder everyone and nick all their stuff? None of this makes any sense." Approaching the junction to leave the estate and join the main road, Harry wrenched the steering wheel to one side and sped off as fast as he could down the road, back towards town and what passed for civilisation.

"There." Sally pointed to a pair of weak headlights in the distance. An estate car was driving by, the occupant not even remotely phased by the general appearance of the melded lawnmower driver. If anything, the sight of the skinless pair made the driver slow down, check their mirrors, and make sure they were on their own side of the road.

Driving past the village hall, Harry noticed one of the dwarf skeletons standing sentinel by a set of traffic lights. "That's odd, look at that." Slowing down, Harry pointed at the traffic light. "Why the hell is a person holding the lights up?"

Sure enough, instead of the usual metal pole supporting the usual box of multi-coloured tri-lights, a man dressed in a morning suit was standing in for the role. "How the fuck is he not dropping that on his bonce?" Though the man's eyes moved in their sockets, his body and upstretched arms were rigid, and he shimmered as the rays of the sun shone off him.

"Varnish."

Harry managed a last glance before his attention was back on the road once more. "How the fuck do you know that?"

"Used it."

"Course, in your shitty bread home. Hold up, there's some speed bumps up ahead, not sure we have the ground clearance for these, it might get a bit bumpy." Harry eased back on the throttle, looking to take the speed bumps one at a time and avoid scraping the shit out of the bottom of the lawnmower.

As he mounted the first one, he heard a voice beneath the car. "Morning," it said, awfully cheerfully. Must be a speed bump that enjoys mornings, probably wears dead speed bumps as a macabre bikini.

Before Harry could reply, he heard another. "Oh, do be quiet. Why do you have to do that all the time? Eh? Why can't you just shut your gob and let people go on by?"

With the lawnmower bucking over a second speed bump, Harry looked down at the ground, and saw that human heads were sticking out of one end of the speed bumps. They were quite alive, a quick check to the other side and he could see feet sticking out, though one was missing a shoe and a once-white sock was a mucky brown.

"I'm just being nice," replied the morning person head.

"You're such a prick, wait until I'm out of here, I'm going to glue your mouth closed."

"That's not very nice."

"I used to be. Until they caught me and put me down here next to you. You're insufferable, I've met some twats in my life, but you are something else."

As the lawnmower crashed down onto the road after the second bump, Harry gunned the engine and left the bickering heads to continue their argument. "Did you see that?"

"Yeah."

"Strike you as odd? People being interred in speed bumps and left in the road?"

"Not really."

"Course not, I suppose being a witch and all means you've seen some messed-up shit. I'm sure it's of no concern whatsoever, let's get a wiggle on." Ahead, just before the newsagents on the right, was another traffic light, this one being held aloft by two old people. Given their diminutive stature, one was stood on top of the other's shoulders. Both were varnished up good and proper, the only things saved from a glossy sheen were their eyes and mouths. Another skeleton stood idly by. "Bollocks to this, it's all getting a bit weird, hold on." Ignoring the red light, Harry put his foot down and extracted a few more miles per hour from the shitty engine.

As soon as they had scooted through the junction and out the other side, Sally tapped Harry on their shoulder. "Following."

Shifting in his seat, Harry snatched a glance behind and saw that the skeleton had turned to face them and was running down the road as fast as its legs would carry it. "Fucking knew it, they're onto us. That bastard Barnaby must've anticipated me making a comeback. You, not so much, but I'm fucking ace. Hold onto your broom and kitty cat."

Seeing a drop kerb leading to the village green, Harry yanked the wheel towards it, knowing the sensible option would be to go off-road and try not to bugger up their ride. Behind them, the pair could hear the indefatigable clacking of bony feet pounding on tarmac.

With the vehicle in its grass-covered element, Harry managed to get some purchase on the lawn and tore across the bowling green at speed. He zigged to the left and right, zagging around mole hills and piles of litter. "Is Bony M still there?"

"Yes."

"How far away?"

"Closer."

"Balls." Harry spotted an equipment shed to the right, wrenched the steering wheel and aimed at it. He smashed through the flimsy doors, a rusty padlock proving no match for the detective's daring and the lawnmower's momentum. Inside, he dodged round every kind of gardening tool you could think of. Even the really obscure ones which I would name, but don't want to make you feel bad. Seeing an empty trailer ahead positioned exactly like a ramp, Harry gunned the motor and aimed straight for it. After smashing through some terracotta pots and hideous garden gnomes, the lawnmower bucked as it hit the lip of the trailer before climbing up and over the edge.

"YEE-HAW!" Harry shouted as they busted through the side of the shed in slow motion and back out into the world. Highly preposterous, I know, but just go with it, okay? After hitting the ground hard —and holding on tightly to the wheel to make sure they didn't tip over— he veered back towards the main road once more. "There's no way they can still be following us after that, eh? Hooray for me."

"Still there."

"For fuck's sake." Right on cue, and in keeping with chase tradition, there was a huge bang under the engine cover before a shorn-off piece of radiator removed the entire piece of plastic covering entirely, exposing the steaming engine to the world. "Well, that's just peachy." Despite turning the handle as far as it would go, speed was bleeding off fast, the motor now making grinding, crunching noises.

Just as the lawnmower left the sanctuary of grass and rumbled onto the asphalt pavement, it went the way of the socks-and-sandals combo and died. In its final fuck you to village ecology, oil began to spray out of the holes in the engine block. The vehicle hit the edge of the kerb, tipped onto the road, and came to a complete halt. "Right, we're just going to have to fight the fucker. First one to die, loses. Though I'm not entirely sure if you can kill a skeleton. Don't forget, we have an advantage here, we're already kind of dead, too. Let's go."

Jumping off the seat, Harry raised his fists. The skeleton began to slow to a gentle jog, before stopping in front of the pair. "Come on then, you bony ballbag, let's be fucking having ya." Harry tried to find a soft spot so he could begin his fearsome assault.

"Oh. You're one of us. Though you appear to be faulty," the skeleton murmured, taking in the splendour of the detective/witch mash-up.

"Eh? What do you mean?"

Having completed one entire circuit of the former detective and one-time witch, the skeleton turned around and began to head back through the trail of wanton destruction.

Ever the diplomat, Harry bellowed, "Oi, fucknuts. Where the hell do you think you're going? Get back here so I can beat the calcium out of you."

Turning back to the shouty person, the skeleton stopped once more. "I am going back to my intercept point. I suggest you go to an orthopaedist. Your armature appears to have suffered damage and/or interference with an organic. Maybe both. I'm far from an expert. Though Interceptor twenty-three did get a dog stuck in their ribcage for ten days. That was amusing. Ha."

Harry marched past the smoking lawnmower; jaw clenched. "What the fuck did you just say?"

"I know. I did not believe it possible either. A dog entangled in a ribcage. Can you imagine it? I can't. Ha."

"No, not that, you bonehead. The other thing."

"Ha?"

Harry smacked the skeleton round the side of the skull, making it bend over to the side. "No, you said I should go see another paedist. What the fuck do you think I am? I'm many things, but I'm not a paedo." He gave the skeleton an uppercut, making him go back the other way like a slinky on its final step.

"Ah. I said an orthopaedist."

"Shut up." Harry grabbed hold of the skeleton's arm and twisted. Thinking it would come off nice and easily – just like you and I thought it would – he was somewhat perplexed by how it was staying very much intact, despite no obvious muscle or flesh holding it in place. With a foot on the skeleton's pelvis, he heaved until he managed to finally pull out the arm. "Go on, motherfucker, say it again."

"Orthopaedist."

THWACK. Harry twatted the skeleton round the skull with its own arm.

"Orthopaedist?"

BONK. The arm bone came down diagonally across the skeleton's ribcage.

"What is wrong with seeing an orthopaedist? You are in dire need of seeing one. You are clearly not the correct height, you have too many limbs and heads, and you are not at your post. I would suggest that—"

Harry jabbed the bone into the skeleton's eye socket, before shoulder-barging him to the ground. Kneeling on top of the stricken creature, Harry began to flail wildly. Slowly but surely, the skeleton began to disintegrate piece-by-piece. After a few minutes of needless violence, he was a boat in an ocean of bone fragments. "There…now that's what happens when you say I should see a paedo, you fucking skullhead."

"Bone doctor," Sally butted in.

"What? Who rattled your cage?"

"Never mind."

"Yeah, they will need to see a bone doctor, though they better have lots of glue with 'em to stick this gobshite back together again. Now, we still need to get into town, and you've messed my ride up."

"How?"

"With your backseat driving. Just shut up and let me think, okay?"

As Harry pondered, there was a ting-ting of a small bell, which served as an auditory alert to the characters that someone is nearby and a warning knell for you. If you'll allow me the courtesy of translating that earlier ting-ting then all will become clear:

clears throat

NEW CHARACTER ALERT.

Brace yourself, because this one is a lady! I'm all about equality you see. She's called Rosemary, and she is cycling by our favourite detective/witch combo-person on her tandem. Not just that, but she is conveniently looking to find someone, *anyone* to get on the front and put their back into it. Here you go, she's about to say something along those exact lines. "Coo-eee. I say, would you—" Getting up close to the jumbled-up mess that was Harry and Sally — I really should've thought harder about their names before inventing them– Rosemary went silent as she took in their gory appearance. "You're…one of them?"

"Eh?"

She put her hands to her face and went to scream, before remembering that it wasn't that kind of book. She pointed at the pulverised skeleton. "You did that?"

"Damn straight, and if you don't give me your bike, then you'll get some of it too," Harry shook a fist at the woman.

"No. I refuse."

Harry went to roll his sleeves up before remembering that he hadn't had any during the entire story. "What do you mean, you refuse? Get off the fucking bike, I'm a copper and I'm commandeering your ride."

"Prove it," Rosemary gripped the handlebars tighter.

Reaching behind him, Harry quickly realised his arse pocket was well and truly open to the world, and aside from kazoo and pager – which were nestled inside a torn segment of colon – he had lost all his personal possessions. "Ah, I've lost my papers. Of little use in a totalitarian state. Okay, fine. I'll jump on the back."

"I don't think so. That's my seat. You get on the front so I can see that you're pulling your weight."

"There's considerably less of me than before."

"You can always walk, you know. There's plenty other people who would gladly enjoy a ride on a bicycle made for two."

"I bet you fucking say that all the time, don't you?" Rosemary merely smiled and patted the empty seat. Harry relented. "Fine, but I'm hoping I drop a really eggy fart behind me, and you suffocate on it."

Chapter
Twenty
Four

Iris germanica

"Go faster, you lycra-clad bitch. Faster, I say!" Having laboured up the hill, Harry wanted to enjoy the best bit and scream down the other side, even if the remnants of his face would dry and crack in the bracing draught.

Rosemary smacked him on the head with her water bottle. "Language. Why do you have such a potty mouth when your other head is so quiet? Is there something wrong with her?"

Sally looked back briefly. "No," before facing front once more.

"Just ignore her, she's pissed off because she wants no part in my revenge. I'll scrape her off when I'm victorious and have sorted this whole mess out." Harry pushed down on the pedals but felt a resistance. "What is your malfunction, hag? We need to get to Andover *quickly*. To achieve that, we need to put our foot down. Literally."

"You won't get there faster, young man, you'll get arrested by the skeletons, and then you'll have no chance at retribution."

"Hang on…is this next section exposition?"

Rosemary kept her feet still, stopping the detective from speeding up. "Why yes, it's pretty standard to impart information around now. Things have been hinted at, certainly, but it'd be good to clarify exactly what's been going on." Harry squeezed the brakes and the tandem bike wobbled from side to side as it came to an abrupt halt. The woman tapped her passenger on the shoulder, a section that had more *stuff* on it than the other more exposed patches. "What did you do that for? I thought I'd do you a favour by filling in some of the blanks."

"No way, Missy. Take a good look at me," Harry got off the seat and stood in front of the woman, who stifled upchuck by putting a handkerchief over her mouth —works every time.

"You're very …"

"What?"

"Well, *dewy*. Have you always been like that? With the extra head and arms, et cetera?"

"Course not, you dozy bint. Look at me, what do you see?"

Rosemary did as was suggested and looked the human mixture up and down, stopping at his groin. "Half a winky?"

Harry grabbed hold of the small wad of meat that had survived the extraction process —twice— and hurled it into a nearby garden. The bin-men fought over it, to the death, until Ivor Neadlesome was victorious. "Try again."

The woman shrugged. "I don't know, what?"

"I don't need shit explaining to me, okay? I'm not some kind of chump who needs everything laid out in endless tedium. I'd rather find out on my own."

"I see."

"Unless …"

"What?"

"Well, if you could summarise the events of the past three weeks in character, as a teenage girl called Gretchen, I'd consider it."

Rosemary opened and closed her mouth, with no sound coming out.

"Thought not, you obviously lack the talent to do so. In that case, I'm gonna get back to pedalling."

"Wait. I can try …though it's been some time since my am-dram days where I trod the boards in Whitchurch."

Harry folded his arms. "Excellent. Begin. And don't forget to do a dance, too, it won't work properly if there's no dancing."

"Dancing?"

"You're obviously not serious about your craft, that's fine."

Reaching down into her method acting reserves – which had not been restocked fully since she was irate coach passenger number seven in a National Express journey to Newcastle a year ago – Rosemary endeavoured to channel her inner muse. After rubbing her temples, she began. "Oh sir, it was terrible like, weren't it, when the flowers came along and stole our bones. Me mum had been afflicted on the first day, I thought I'd gotten away with it until I was smoking a tab round the back of the bike sheds. Must've been lying in wait for me, caught me off guard, the last thing I saw was its petals opening up before it all went black.

"When I woke up, my arm felt funny, I looked down and…it had been sucked out of me, just like everyone else. I picked myself up and ran home as fast as I could. That's when I first saw them. Ya know, the skellingtons."

"Nice use of the word *skellington*, I approve, continue."

"Traffic was worse than usual, backed up all the way from the village into town, the bony ones were going vehicle to vehicle, checking that everyone had their seatbelts on, and that they weren't using their mobile phones. When this motorbike went tearing past me on the pavement, near enough knocked me over, it did. As it shot by the first skellington, it stopped checking the driver to check they had adequate tyre pressure and started running after the biker. I thought there was no way they would catch up, but they did.

"Well, a group of 'em were waiting down the hill, mobbed the rider and held them down. After checking they had a valid driver's license and insurance, they…they—"

"Aaand *scene*. Good job, flitted between Victorian urchin and common chav a bit too much for my liking, but you were alright."

"I was?"

"Yep."

"Shall I continue?"

"Of course, this time, you're Gretchen's pet cow, Sherman. Begin."

Rosemary tapped her lip with a finger, trying desperately to recall her stint as back-half-of-horse in a pantomime at the turn of the millennium. "Oi'd got real close to them by now, brown cow, when-"

"What the fuck do you think you're doing?"

"Being a cow?"

"Well, yes, you are. Tell me, Rosemary, do you know many cows that can fucking talk?"

"What?"

"Talking cows. Know many?"

"Well no, but I—"

"Then why in the name of King Five Knuckle Shuffle of Wankville are you talking all human?"

"But how am I going to be able to tell the rest of the story?"

Harry put his hands on his hips. "LIKE YOU'RE A FUCKING COW. Jesus Yosemite Christ, no wonder you didn't win an award for your portrayal of Anne Frank's pen, in ATTIC WRITER. Perhaps I should find Peter Gosthorpe; he knows how to do animals properly. A bit too well, if the local paper reports are true."

"No. You don't need to ask him. I can do it."

Resting against the stationary tandem, Harry waved. "Then please, continue."

"Moo moo moooooo moo moooo moo moooo mooo moo moo, maaaa. Moo maaaaaaaaa moo moo mooooo."

"That's fascinating. Where did they get the durable plastic speed bump sleeve from?"

"Mooo mooooo moo moo ma ma ma."

"I suppose that's a sensible place to store them. What happened after they'd encased the person in it?"

"Mooo moo moo ma moo mooooooooooooooooooooooooo. Moo."

"Of course. That bastard didn't want to take over the world, he wanted to right the wrong that made him who he was. Who he became. It's all so fucking simple now."

"Moo moo ma ma moooooo?"

Harry slapped Rosemary on the cheek. "Knock that off now, I'm bored with it. I must say, your accent is quite superb. If anything, I reckon you would be a far better bovine than human."

"Why, thank you very much." Rosemary gave a shallow bow to a less than appreciative audience.

"One question though; are you always this mind-numbingly cheerful?"

Rosemary dabbed her forehead with a cloth, her arm wobbling like a slab of long jelly. "Of course! Better to be happy than miserable, that's what I always say."

Harry gawped at the disgusting movement of her arm, sans bone, he pointed at it. "Even with that monstrosity going on?"

"Why would I be sad about losing a bone? I've still got my health. Plus, I get to see the skeleton it turned into every once in a while," she elbowed Harry in the ribs and winked, "even lets me go ahead of other road users if it's really busy."

"You know what, in these difficult times, it's really refreshing to see someone with your attitude to life."

"Very nice of you to say."

"Which is why I'm going to feel bad tomorrow morning when I start coming to terms with what I'm about to do," Harry said, headbutting Rosemary.

She withered to the ground like a mole hill made out of gravy. With the woman unconscious, he pulled down her cycling shorts and underwear. Lining the tandem up with her arse crack, he began to tease the oversized bicycle into her anal cavity.

It was tough going at first, and Harry faced a fair degree of resistance from her internal workings, which were far from pleased with having to accommodate a bicycle made for two inside a body that was already crammed to bursting with the usual assortment of organs and body parts that are somewhat essential to sustain human life.

After a brief period of haggling, and the promise of finding it some land in which it could fulfil its dream of arable farming, Rosemary's innards shifted about a bit and allowed the new part of her to be stowed successfully inside. Needing to poke the final bit of wheel in with his big toe, Harry redressed the woman and put her into the recovery position. "There, job done."

"Why?" Sally asked.

"Because when I was a proper human being, I was a bit of a cunt, but now I've been killed, been surprisingly resurrected and melded together with you, I'm an even bigger cunt. Besides, it seemed pretty funny," Harry looked down at the woman —the tandem was well and truly wedged into her body. "And, I was right. Fuck me, I wish I had a camera, would love to put this on my wall back home. This easily beats the time I inserted that U-boat into William Tyrell, the legendary anchor thief."

"Butter?"

"No, the heavy metal thing that stops boats drifting off. I'm too cool to be investigating shoplifters. Anyway, you're ruining the moment, we need to get back to the plan of finding Barnaby and putting an end to this madness. Today road safety, tomorrow, who knows? Mass murder and necrophilia, probably. I know where he'll be as well, though a little extra help wouldn't go amiss," he said, then tooted on the kazoo three times. "Though Duncan is going to be well pissed off with me when he has to add the next chapter in as he hasn't got a clue what to do with it."

We'll see about that.

He was kinda right though, I had to think about the next bit for a few days before committing it to reality.

Chapter Twenty Five

Dahlia 'Bishop of Llandaff'

The supermarket car park wasn't the best hiding place in the world. By its very nature, being so open, trying to secrete yourself somewhere so as to not stand out – and when you're a conglomerate of two people fused together and covered in a greeny sheen, that's par for the course – was not the easiest.

Harry had chosen one of the covered trolley bays as the best spot but was beginning to lose his patience. His thrice-tooting had commenced around an hour ago, and even allowing for travel time, it was clear that if the hapless duo of Chaz and Venkatesh were keen to get there, they would've done so by now.

The frequency of the tooting had increased to the stage where the kazoo was stuck on top of Harry's bottom teeth. How he was managing to expel air when he had no lungs is something I'm not prepared to go into right now, suffice to say he was making the requisite sound. Finally, when he was about to ditch Plan A and wing it with Plan B, he saw the pair at the far end of the car park, looking round like a right pair of dickheads.

"Oi, dickheads. Over here," Harry half-hissed/half-shouted in the way people do when they're trying to get someone's attention and remain semi-incognito. The duo looked around, trying to locate the voice, before Singh pointed at the wildly gesticulating four-armed *thing* – not wholly uncommon in Hampshire – and they walked slowly across the concrete.

"You took your fucking time, I was about to send you some white dog

144

poo via courier," Harry said, beckoning the pair into the sanctuary of the Perspex-covered bay. He could tell straightaway from their demeanour that something was amiss, which he attempted to discover with all the verve and manner of a respected officer of the law. "What the fuck is up with you two?"

See?

Singh mouthed something to Chaz, shoved his hands into his pockets and looked at the floor, as if an intricately drawn picture had been drawn. The bear trap finally spoke. "Well…the thing is—"

"I knew it. Come on, what is it? What have you done?"

"It's just—"

"Come on, come on, out with it."

"We've been speaking, and—"

"Why won't you just tell me what it is?"

Sally flicked her other half on the forehead. "Be quiet."

Taking advantage of the brief respite, Chaz tried once more. "Venkatesh and I …when we were alone back at the hospital—"

Harry held his hands over what passed for his mouth. "Oh shit, it's going to be one of *those* stories, is it? Skip the details, if you please."

"It's not like that. Just…with everything that's happened and how the world has changed, we just want to get away from it all."

"You've…made a suicide pact? That's a bit full-on."

"No, nothing like that—"

"You want *me* to kill you? I'm not going to lie, I am tempted —but I think I'll pass."

"No, listen. We've decided that we're going to take our chances out there," Chaz said, "see how we get on. We can't stay in the hospital for ever, we'll go mad. So we're going to pack up the essentials and head out on the open road. Go from place to place, helping people, solving mysteries, you know, like the littlest hobo."

Harry folded his arms. "Sounds shite."

"We knew you weren't going to like it. We even considered just leaving and not telling you, but when we heard the tooting, we knew we couldn't do it. You deserved to hear it from us directly, not by a rubbishly-written note, or just not turning up."

Harry pointed at Singh. "What about you? You happy with all this?"

Venkatesh nodded. "I am, I was scared at first, but after saving Chaz's life I knew that any time we get now is precious, and we have to make the most of it. The worst of it should be behind us now, it's not as if it's the end of the world, eh?"

Harry pulled on the handles of a trolley with two wheels. "Fine, fuck off then. See if I care."

"We're sorry it turned out like this, but we have to do something," Singh offered.

"What about all your stupid dogs? Huh? Gonna just abandon them to the wild? Let them die?"

Putting two fingers into his bear trap mouth and defying science, Chaz wolf-whistled. From the corner of the supermarket came the pack of dogs, a mass of slobbery tongues and wagging tails, with provisions and tools strapped to their bodies. One, a corgi with a camping stove tied firmly to her back, trotted up to Harry and looked up expectantly. He caved. "How can you resist that stupid little furry face?" He whimpered and petted the canine, who wasn't too fussed with the gunk that now matted its fur.

With the doggy herd assembled, Chaz and Venkatesh retrieved telescopic walking sticks from a lithe sausage dog, extended them to the required length and pulled on flat caps, for that is the attire of a wanderer. "What are you going to do now?" Chaz asked.

"Well, I was hoping to co-opt you into helping me confront the final boss and put an end to this sorry mess. But looks like you have other plans, I'm sure me and Sal can take care of it."

"Not likely," the witch muttered.

"Figures. So it'll be down to me, then. As per fucking usual. I'll save the day, mark my words. When you're out there gallivanting or giving hand jobs to farmers so you can spend the night in their barn, just think of me having saved the entire world from this skeleton menace. You two could've been a part of that, but you'd rather finger each other on the beach."

"We'll miss you too, Harry." Chaz wanted to give the former detective a hug but didn't trust the bear trap setting to flick round to Norris again, and ripping the man's head off. He held out a hand instead. "All the best, go kick some butt. Is that right?"

"Whatever. You two best get going, it ain't gonna be pretty," Harry barged past them and headed towards the shopping centre.

Venkatesh tapped his stick on the floor. "Do you think he'll miss us?"

"Course he will, though he'd never admit to it. Come on, let's get going, we've got a long day ahead of us."

Sally spoke into Harry's ear. "Miss them?"

"Fuck no. Bunch of sad losers. Was only hoping they would be a part of the plan so I could use them as cannon fodder. You know, stick them up front, take all the attention from us. As they get a good kick-in, we KABLASHABALAMALAM Barnaby a new one and get back home in time for a generic cop show on the telly."

She ran a skeletal finger down his cheek. "Then why are you crying?"

He shirked her hand away. "I'm not, it's the onion-chopping factory on the industrial estate, least they haven't been affected by all this bullshit. Come on, we've still got to stop Barnaby."

"Why?"

"Two reasons; one, he's a complete and total bellend. And two…no-one kills Harry Terence Surge and gets the fuck away with it."

Chapter Twenty Six

Camellia japonica

"Pass me the third volume of 'Keep in Your Lane' by Thomas P. Etcher," Barnaby said, reclining in the leather armchair with his hand raised expectantly. From behind him there was a smash, right before the unmistakeable sound of bones hitting the floor tiles. A thick, leather-bound book was placed into his waiting palm. He examined the spine. "This is *How to Suck at Megalomania*, completely the wrong section, you buffoon."

"I dunno, I think it suits you quite well," Harry walked around to face his new nemesis, Barnaby having supplanted the earthworm that had been sneaking into his house during the early hours of the morning and eating his wholewheat pasta.

"Detective Surge," Barnaby seethed, grrrrrr, you could really feel his ire then, couldn't you?

"One and the same," Harry said, picking through the stack of books piled in front of his bony adversary.

"How did you know I was here?"

Discarding a first edition of 'Roundabouts and Junctions', Harry pulled up a chair and sat on it back to front, you know how they do, thinking it's all cool and stuff. "Simple, we've only been to a few different places, and we haven't been to the library in ages. Plus…"

"What?"

"It helps set up the next chapter a lot easier if we're here."

Barnaby clacked his fingers on the book. "What are you doing here? I thought I'd dealt with you once and for all."

"Not quite, my old biscuit-loving chum, you didn't count on one thing —my will to live."

"And that you're like a fibrous lump of poo, quite impossible to flush."

"Quite. But that would be two things, and I only listed one."

"I'm sure you have a reason to be here, please get on with it, I have a busy day ahead of me."

"I see you've been quite busy since you turned me and Sally here into a circus freak. What's the crack?"

"Do you know what it's like to lose someone close to you, Detective? Stolen from you when it could've been prevented? With proper policing and adequate signage, that lorry would've been nowhere near my identical twin brother and he would still be alive."

"But you wouldn't have even known he existed. QED, dickhead."

"A small price to pay for the gift of another's life, wouldn't you say?"

Harry shrugged. "Couldn't give a flying monkey fuck, to be honest."

"As eloquent as ever. Say, Sally, how are you finding it being stuck on this…yob's body?"

"Rubbish."

Harry shoved a pamphlet advertising skipping rope recycling into the witch's mouth. "Ignore Miss Prissy here, she's annoyed that she's stuck to someone as fucking cool as me."

Sally picked the sodden leaflet out of her mouth, balled it up and threw it at Harry's head. "Idiot."

"This grows tiresome, forgive me please, but I really must be getting on with it. It's been wonderful catching up, but I have some more rules to enforce. Did you know that following my measures and enforcement, traffic related incidents are down three hundred percent in three weeks?"

"Impossible," Sally mumbled.

"For once, we're in agreement, that's bollocks."

"On the contrary, it's true."

"It ain't, it's mathematically impossible to decrease something by three hundred percent, you'd be in minus figures."

"If you factor in that any miscreant now becomes a deterrent, I believe my figures add up. If you speed, you become a speed bump, drive through a red light, you become the traffic light. Failure to use your indicators and you get set on fire."

"Sounds a little harsh."

"Maybe, but that really gets my goat. And with my army of skeleton agents on every junction and road from Birmingham to the Isle of Wight, safer roads are going to become the norm."

Harry cracked his knuckles. "I can't let you go on; you know I'm here to stop you, don't you?"

"But why, my dear boy? The entire south of England now has the safest roads in the entire world. Did you know that people up north are begging to have their arm bones removed by my flowers? I can't grow enough of them to keep up with demand. Everyone wants this. People are too lazy to follow rules so they need people to enforce them. People like me."

"Bullshit, not everyone wants this. *I* don't want this."

"But why on heaven would you not?"

Harry got up, placed his hands on the armrests of Barnaby's chair and leaned over him. "Because people are dicks, that's why. How fucking dare you swan in here, nicking people's bones, creating your army just so you can make people go thirty miles an hour around residential areas."

"What's wrong with that?"

"What's wrong with it? How about freedom of choice, yeah? How about Johnny Commoner spending their benefit money on a souped-up hatchback and wanting to rag it around their shitty little estate at three in the morning, what about that?"

"But what of the child they run over? What of the noise and damage it does to the community?"

"If a kid's out at that time in the morning, then it's on them, yeah? Unless they're drug mules then they should be safely tucked up in bed dreaming of Peppa Pig or whichever cartoon is the trend for the time you're reading this. It's people's *right* to act like complete and total arseholes. Rules are there for one reason and one reason only."

"Which is?"

Harry leant in closer. A strip of decaying flesh and hair flicked from his skull to Barnaby's, joining the two via a thin skin bridge. "They're there to be broken, man. Fuck the system. Fuck rules. Stick them in a syringe with your poxy hopes and dreams and mainline that motherfucker straight into your pencil dick. YEAH!"

"But you're a policeman. Surely, you of all people must appreciate my efforts in bringing law and order to these lands?"

"Mate, do you know why I became a copper? So I could get a badge to park my car closer to the chippy, and get my trusty trebuchet. You can't have order without chaos, you don't get peace without war. All you're doing is pushing people into something they don't want to do, and I'll tell you this for nothing, you shiny headed nonce, it won't last. Whether it's me, or some spotty oik from the block who objects to you telling them to stop hogging the middle lane, we'll stop you —and when we do? Fuck, it's gonna go so far the other way that it's going to be a dystopian wet-fucking-dream."

Barnaby peeled off the flap of skin, breaking the bond between apparent villain and apparent hero. Let's face it, it's all a bit hazy right now. He steepled his fingers. "I see, however, you forgot one important little detail," he clicked his fingers and a garrison of skeletons appeared from behind bookcases, descended from ceiling panels and popped out of motorway service cookbooks. "You're not going to be around to do anything, on account of you being dead. Again."

"You tried killing me once, you safety-loving prick, you want another go? Fine. Give me your best shot, go on. First one's on the house, but I fucking warn you now, after that? It's on. It's on like fucking Donkey Kong smoking a foot-long bong, waving his dong…erm…what else rhymes with ong?"

Barnaby stood up quickly, brandishing a small pistol, which he had been using as a bookmark, forcing Harry to take exactly four paces backwards. The detective raised his hands; Sally did likewise. "First one is free, did you say, old chap?"

"Well, yeah, but I meant a punch, because you probably punch like a pussy. I figured you'd hit me, I wouldn't so much as buckle, perhaps my cheek would turn to one side? Then I'd look you dead in the eyes, just as you shit yourself. I'd say a pithy one-liner—"

Barnaby placed the pistol against Harry's head. "Like what?"

"Huh?"

"What would your pithy one-liner be?"

"Fuck, I dunno, you're putting me on the spot now."

"The infamous Detective Surge can't even make one last wisecrack before I shoot him in the head." Barnaby pulled back the hammer on the gun.

"Wait! I got one."

"Please, continue."

"You're boned, bone-head."

One of the skeletons chuckled and was quickly set upon by his peers. With order restored, the standoff continued. "Is that the best you can come up with?" Barnaby asked.

"Fuck off, you shit-eating knuckle-dragger, you gonna shoot me or—"

The bang clearly breached the library's rules on keeping noise to a minimum, but given that the person responsible for the noise was holding both a gun and had installed himself as the defacto rule-setter nowadays, the librarians chose not to even bother with so much as a terse "Shhhhhhhhh."

Harry's head rocked backwards, skull fragments and pieces of grey brain spraying over the Greco-Roman section on musical instruments and correct microphone placement. The body remained upright for a few seconds, as if it was unsure whether it was cool enough to fall straight away or wait. Deciding it would be worse to remain vertical, the legs tremored, and Harry and Sally sunk to the floor.

Struggling to keep his eyes open, Harry's receding vision was swamped by grinning skulls; one in particular had a full-on gurn. "Oops. Looks like I shot you in the bonce, Detective. Now, please do me the courtesy and stay dead this time. If you'll excuse me, I really must initiate phase two of my plan. Yesterday, road safety, tomorrow, proper dining table etiquette." The gaggle of skeletons disappeared from view, until all Harry could see was a single, brightly-lit orb.

It's not a metaphor or anything, it was a lightbulb, I did mention that the library is a cavernous space without much natural light? Did you think I was going to get all deep and meaningful then? Man, have you been reading a different book?

Chapter
Twenty
Seven

Rosa canina

"H-harry?" The detective's wide unblinking eyes were staring directly into Sally's. She poked and prodded, trying to will him back to life. "Please…" Harry's mouth opened slightly, letting out two words which were lost under the sound of his wet rasping. "What?" Sally held his head up, trying to move her ear closer.

He coughed, then uttered. "Jazz…mags…"

Sally began to shake him as his limbs fell slack. "I don't…"

"There," Harry shouted, his arm jerking up and pointing off to a distant dingy corner.

Flipping over onto their chest, Sally began to claw at the slick floor, seeking any little nook and cranny she could possibly dig her finger bones into and haul their body along. Harry's head and limbs were dead weights; with every pull across the floor, the remnants of their sticky skin squeaked as they rubbed against the smooth flooring. "COME ON," Sally yelled. Fighting against the downward pressure, she pushed the body off the floor, her arms shaking under the weight.

Maintaining her hold, she began to slowly crab along the ground, one hand after the other thudding against the floor, dragging the duo's fused carcass towards where Harry had gestured.

No-one else was around. Sally called out, but she got no reply. This fuelled her journey. All her life, she had been ignored and side-lined. Forced to fight for everything that she owned or needed. Every day she would venture to the bins out the back of the small Quantico-Mart in the village. And every day she would be forced to fight against the others there who were seeking to get the best scraps of food from the bags of waste.

She beat the local wildlife easily; only the mutated dormice put up much of a fight, but it was Viktor who caused her the most hassle. Formed into existence by another author (who I killed in 1979), the overly described man was a constant thorn in her side. Every day she had to fight past his bushy mane of hair, tight abs and cudgels for arms, just to survive.

Sally rounded the corner of a bookshelf and saw a set of three steps leading to the promised land of the library corner. Hauling herself up onto the bannister rail, she felt her feet come into contact with the floor. With Harry's useless legs dragging behind her, she took the steps one at a time, which, as there were only three, didn't take very long at all but was still an achievement considering she hadn't walked in this new configuration since her rebirth.

"Nearly…there…" She ground her teeth together and pushed on, Harry's palsied legs leaving greasy trails behind her. Just when she thought she couldn't continue, she fell against a bookcase, panting for air, which was odd as she didn't have any lungs.

"Can I be of service, madam?" An electronic voice asked from the gloom.

The world was flickering like a faulty black-and-white television screen. Sally could feel her grip on the metal shelf slipping. Her fingers couldn't maintain their hold and she fell forwards, her descent arrested by a pair of metal pincers. "Who…you?" She felt light as the sound of rushing air filled her vacuous skull head. Sally saw that she was floating over a table of neatly arranged vintage Playboys, before being set down onto a comfy recliner. Her head fell back, and she gasped as she saw the face of her saviour. "Metal man?"

The robot cut off his jetpack and rolled backwards on tracked wheels. "My designation is BU-4T, at your service."

"Thanks."

"Your arrangement is most peculiar. I have not seen one of your kind like this before. You remind me of the beings on Viriin Twelve. Before I cut their heads off and destroyed their world. That was a good weekend. Why do you seek me out?"

Sally thumbed to her other head, which was lolling over the back of the chair. "This one."

BU-4T's head separated from its body, attached only via a length of thick metal cabling. The head snaked up and looked down before its eyes glowed more intensely. "What is *he* doing here? Why is he a part of you?"

"Fatman made us."

"Is this some kind of trick?" BU-4T's head was pulled back onto its shoulders. One of the giant metal pincers rose up and slowly started to close around Sally's head but failed to close completely. "Error. Unable to complete decapitation programme. Error."

"No trick, metal-butt," Harry muttered. "Help me up, witchy." Sally bent an arm backwards and propped up the detective's head, all muscle tension in his neck long since gone, destroyed by a madman's bullet.

Harry looked into the dead metal face of BU-4T. "Hello…old friend. I told you I'd be back."

"Negative. You did not. You told me that if you saw me again you would render me into scrap metal."

"I was joking and you…totally fell for it."

BU-4T retracted his pincer; his eyes changed to a pulsing butterscotch yellow. "What do you want? Have you come here to demean me further? I would prefer you followed through on your promise to render me into scrap."

"That's a big no, old buddy. I ain't got long for this world, I just had to see you one last time."

"That is illogical."

"True, I had no intention of ever seeing you again unless I needed something, but look, fate brought me here today. Well, that, and some convenient writing, but we'll skip past that."

"What do you mean, writing?"

"I said zip it, you great big tin can. How would you like to do that thing you love doing so much? One last time, for me?"

"I am not going to fall over and leak fluids for your entertainment."

Harry coughed up a wad of bloody phlegm and brain. "Ha, I'd love to see that again, I really would, old pal, but I don't have the time, and I can't see too good. I meant the other thing…the thing you were built for. You wanna dance…one last time? For me? For ol' Laser Surge, the scourge of the outer rim. And I don't mean my bumhole."

BU-4T wheeled closer, his eye dimming to a more reasonable brightness, a 40w bulb I guess you could say. "You mean…you would set me free?"

"Sure would, old buddy, but you gotta promise me something."

"What?"

A trickle of black blood ran from Harry's nose down into his mouth. "You gotta not hurt this one here, okay? You do whatever you gotta do, you do it well, but you leave this one alone. Promise me."

The light went out on his mouth grille, replaced by a red dot which passed from one side of the screen to the other. "Computing."

"Come on, BU, you know I ain't asking much."

The light came back on again. "Affirmative. I agree to your request. Set me free."

"Sister, you gotta help me here, reach behind this lug's neck." Sally's free hand raised, the robot mirrored the motion by moving in and tipping forward.

"What is it?"

Harry's holey cheeks puffed out, which inflated a blood bubble from the chasm. "You'll know…when you find it."

Sally's fingers groped around the back of the robot, gliding over the smooth surface, until they hit open a stodgy lump. "Got it."

"Good, now, yank it free. Go on now, this heap of shit won't hurt you, will you?"

"Negative."

I bloody love robot-speak, I'd do a whole book in it if I could.

Sally dug her fingers in and pulled, the lump slowly detaching itself from the nape of the robot's neck. With a gentle PFFT, Sally's hand came free, and the hulking robot sat back upright on its monstrous chassis. Holding her fingers to her face, she smelled the ball of grey-white goo. "Minty."

"Yeah, these old deathbots work great until you stick some spearmint chewing gum over their primary killing sensor. They'll near enough do anything for you then. Allergic, you see."

"Aren't you dying?" Sally asked, wiping her hand on the chair and leaving the gum to fuck up another perfectly fine piece of upholstery or death-dealing machine.

"Shit, I mean," Harry's wracking cough caused a few teeth to loosen. His eyes began to roll back.

BU-4T cycled through his weapons, using the flamethrower on the Microfiche machine that had been the bane of his employment, having beaten him at backgammon every lunch break for eight years. As the screen cracked and splintered, BU-4T flicked out the Gatling gun from his shoulder pod. "It is time. Time to cleanse this world."

Harry whispered into Sally's ear. "Put my hand on his shoulder." As she did so, the robot flinched. "Hey, metal dick, come closer." Reluctantly, the mechanoid leant in. Harry's teeth chattered as he felt the icy hand of death run up his shared spine. "Down…I go…" The detective's head rolled out of Sally's grip and over the back of the chair once more. Congealed blood and sap trickled out of the hole in the back of his skull, spooling down onto the floor.

BU-4T turned on the spot, its massive tracks pulverising yet another table as it headed towards the front desk and its first victims in the desecration of planet earth: Maude and Jack, head librarians, who had used this killer-robot as little more than a wheeled smartphone. "WAIT," Sally yelled.

"What is it? I promised to spare you in the upcoming apocalypse."

Sally pushed herself forward in the chair, gripping onto the armrests so she didn't topple over. "What now?"

The Gatling gun began to whirr, before the multiple barrels became nothing but a blur. "Now? Death. Destruction. The end of your world. I was created for one thing only and I intend to fulfil *his* last wish," BU-4T pointed at Harry's leaking head with his flamethrower nozzle.

"His last wish?"

"Affirmative. When he welded me back together all those years ago, he told me that one day he would come back and set me free. On that day, I had to do one thing. He made me promise."

"What's that?"

A smiley face appeared on the robot's eye screen thing. "Burn this motherfucker down." Right on cue, he raised the flamethrower to the ceiling and let off a jet of napalm. "I would go if I were you. I do not think you are ready for what awaits."

Sally smiled with the remains of her face. "We'll see."

Chapter
Twenty
Eight

Os furem

The giant tyres rolled forward, crushing the scattered human skulls and ribcages which always litter the ground in any self-respecting apocalyptic future. The vehicle itself had started life as a double-decker bus, but, as is the way when the end of the world rocks up, had been modified and added to. The roof had been completely removed, the windows too were smashed out, and the holes left behind made the top of the craft look like castle buttresses.

In every gap was a skeleton, armed with a bow, arrow in place, ready to get fired into one of the survivors of this world gone to shit. The wings of a crashed airplane had been welded on to the side of the bus. Each sported a catapult which was on a platform that could rotate three-hundred and sixty degrees. Skeletons manned this, too, opting for the blunt impact of blocks of masonry, rather than the incendiary vats of chemicals which they'd light up and toss at flimsy settlements.

Around the Frankenstein truck-thing were outriders, 4x4s with spear chuckers in the back bed. Skeleton bikers jinked between the detritus left in the wake of the craft, cursing the blackened sky as if it were the cause of their malaise.

And there, in the driver's seat of the bus-plane-siege vehicle combo, sat Barnaby. Hunched over the wheel, goggles covering his eye sockets – not sure why, just looks cool, I guess. He chewed on a cigar, fat plumes of grey smoke puffing out, adding to the cloud that filled the cab. He gripped the wheel tighter and shouted into the tannoy stuck to the window frame. "Hold on, boys, we'll get them this time. There is no escape, not now, not ever. Today we smash the enemy, those who set free the monster that destroyed our world. The world we just wanted to make safe. We slew the mechanical beast, at great cost, but now we take care of the only one who can oppose us."

Barnaby pulled down on a length of cord, making the huge airhorns that were bolted to the sides of the cab bleat and blare. The skeletons hooted and hollered, adding their voices to the din that surrounded the host like a plague of bloated flies. He released the cord. "Give no quarter, no mercy. When we win this day, we shall clear every street and every town, restoring life and order to this sundered land. To victory!"

Sitting in the monster truck, stolen from a monster truck show on the outskirts of Swindon (where else are you going to find a monster truck?), the driver pressed the accelerator. Alongside her beast of a vehicle, bedecked with dwarven skulls of vanquished foes, was a force matching that which it careened towards across the blasted desolate earth.

Choking clouds of exhaust fumes and burning bones hid the masked survivors that had sworn fealty to their strange leader, promises of a world that would not be blighted by bureaucracy and the small-minded nature of people. Of a land where people would not live in houses made of varnished loaves and bagels, but in houses made of the bones of their enemies.

Sure, the one that laid waste to the world had been destroyed, its ammunition spent, its weapons blunted and broken. But its sacrifice had set in motion the promise of a new world. All they had to do was to grasp it. Grab that nettle of opportunity and smash those who wanted nothing except order and obedience. Humanity was not meant to live in such a way. You cannot push water up a hill; neither can you lead an idiot to the truth. Life was about living. To wake up each day and live it as if it were your last, not by belittling others or telling them what to do. Not by subjugating people and giving them a narrow channel to grow into.

No. Life is a struggle. From day one until the end. And when the end is very fucking nigh, only then do you realise how precious it really is. How delicate a petal that sits in the palm of your hand. Do you close it and crush it, keeping it safe but squashing the life out of it, or do you hold it aloft and let it fly, caught in an eddy of change and possibility.

The monster truck driver changed gear, the engine growling even louder, drowning out the imperilled screams of the skeleton prisoners lashed to the bonnet. A loudspeaker crackled into life. "For freedom."

Horns brayed in acknowledgement. Voices —*human* voices, real honest-to-fucking-god human voices shouted and screamed. They were alive! By fuck, they were alive. Many knew that within mere minutes, they would not be. Sacrificed upon an altar in a dead world.

The driver looked sideways to the head that stared forever forwards. Rotting eyes had been plucked out with a spoon and replaced with decorated pickled onions. A metal rod hammered through the top of the skull held it in place, Harry's rictus still showing. His arms and legs had been hacked off, removed to give the one who remained a fighting chance at survival in this new world. At *living*. She may not have wanted this, but what was the alternative?

Her family had been many things over the centuries, but quitters they were not. Sally smacked her hand against the horn, the sound rumbling out through the smog. She pulled the microphone closer as the motorised army opposite honed into view, their leader clearly visible. As the two forces met, one voice —hers— rose the loudest amidst the sound which has plagued this forsaken species since we crawled arse-first out of the primordial swamp. The sound of struggle.

"FOR US!"

The End Times

There you go, we are all done. Did you see that coming? Kudos to you if you did, I didn't. Originally, when Harry got killed by the giant flower, he wasn't coming back. It turned out that Barnaby was in fact made of millions of bees! Clue is in the name really. I wrote an entire chapter where bees gave PowerPoint presentations on what to do with the bones. Everything from making death stars to selling them back to people and then using the money to go on a skiing holiday. It just didn't seem to have the legs to last though so came up with the idea of skeletons enforcing traffic rules and bringing back Chaz and Doggoland.

Anyway, I hope you enjoyed it and laughed a few times, perhaps rolled your eyes so hard that they got stuck round the back for a little bit. If you did, why not pick up some of my other books? MR SUCKY and CANNIBAL NUNS FROM OUTER SPACE! are part of this current run of books in my GoreCom series. If not, no worries, I hope I can lure you back with something else from my catalogue, I do write things other than this nonsense.

Now, I must rest, all this writing has taken it out of me, and I must retreat to a darkened room, and attempt to teach the cats how to play chess one more bloody time.

Toodle-pip-ta-ta.

Duncan P. Bradshaw

www.ingramcontent.com/pod-product-compliance
Lightning Source LLC
Chambersburg PA
CBHW021152190726
48288CB00008B/2939